IN SPRITE OF HERSELF

A PARANORMAL MYSTERY ADVENTURE

MONSTERS OF JELLYFISH BEACH 6

WARD PARKER

MAD MANGROVE MEDIA

CONTENTS

CHAPTER I
TOOTH FAIRY TALE

It was my first fancy date with Matt, at a place so upscale that he wore his only sport coat and parked his beat-up pickup truck a block away so the valet service wouldn't see it.

I had just been served my appetizer of escargot when my phone rang. It was the organization devoted to creatures even stranger than buttered snails: the Friends of Cryptids Society of the Americas. I sent the call to voicemail.

As we ate and sipped our expensive wine, my phone kept buzzing from calls and texts.

"Why are you frowning?" Matt asked. The night was so special, he had even trimmed his beard and shaved his neck. I felt honored.

"The Society is bugging me about something. I don't want them to ruin this evening."

Matt's phone buzzed. As a reporter, he never ignored his

phone, in case a story lead came in. He shrugged sheepishly and glanced at the screen.

"The Society texted me," he said. "I didn't think they had my number. They want you to call them right away because of an emergency."

"Really? I'm so sick of them."

My phone buzzed again. I sighed and answered it.

"We've been alerted that a crested mouth sprite has been killed, and we need to collect evidence," Mrs. Lupis said. "The crested mouth sprite is exceedingly rare, and we've never examined one, alive or dead."

"A crested what?"

"Mouth sprite. Otherwise known as a tooth fairy. We need you to collect the remains so we can do a necropsy. As a nurse for supernaturals, you're perfect for the job."

"Where is it?"

"In a home in Jellyfish Beach. A father apparently shot the creature while it was about to take his child's tooth."

"How do you know this?" I asked.

"We have our methods."

"I can't just barge into a stranger's house."

"You will, and you must hurry. The police have already arrived after a neighbor reported the shotgun blast. As far as the Society is concerned, this is a murder, even if the police don't believe so."

"But I'm a nurse and a botanica owner. They won't let me take evidence."

"You are now unofficially an agent of the Florida Fish and Wildlife Conservation Commission."

"How am I supposed to—"

"Excuse me, madam," said the restaurant manager, who had suddenly appeared at the table. "This is for you."

He handed me an envelope. Inside was a badge for the FWC.

"How do you do this stuff?" I asked Mrs. Lupis.

"I told you we have our methods. Please go to the home at 12 Barnacle Way immediately. We've paid for your dinner for you."

The server appeared with takeout boxes containing the entrees we had ordered but hadn't been served.

"Your bill has been settled," she said haughtily. "Including a very minimal gratuity."

Matt pulled out some bills and dropped them on the table as we left. I wasn't surprised my Society handlers had under-tipped; they weren't fully dialed in on human etiquette.

THE HOME WAS in a middle-class neighborhood with lots of cars parked in driveways, because Florida homes lack basements, and garages are used to store everything except cars.

A patrol car was parked on the street in front of the address Mrs. Lupis gave me, a home where one of the cars in the driveway sat atop concrete blocks instead of wheels, and crab traps were piled in the side yard. It was obviously a neighborhood without an HOA.

Matt pushed through the front door that had been left ajar, with me right behind. Our plan was for him to distract everyone with a reporter's questions while I found and collected the sprite's remains.

"I'll have to cite you for reckless discharge of a firearm indoors and endangering a minor," the officer said, a young woman who stared at the homeowner with an expression that said she wanted to discharge her own firearm at him.

The homeowner was a tall, shirtless, inebriated man with greasy hair, a potbelly, and a shotgun cradled in his arms.

"I told you I had to kill a bat in my son's room," he said in a surly Southern accent.

"You could have called critter control instead of shooting it in your son's bedroom while he was sleeping."

"It coulda been a vampire bat."

"It was the tooth fairy," said a six-year-old boy with a mullet haircut who popped up from a chair in front of the TV. "Now, I won't get my money."

"There's no such thing as the—" the father said before stopping himself. "The fairy will come back, and you'll get yer money."

I flashed my brand-new FWC badge at the cop and headed for the bedrooms.

"Hey, what are you doing?" she asked me.

"I have to check the bat carcass. There's been an outbreak of rabies."

"See?" the father said. "That thing coulda bitten my son. I'm a hero, in fact."

"You didn't have to shoot it with a twelve-gauge shotgun," Matt said.

"You mind yer own business, you little twerp. Who are you, anyway?"

"I'm a reporter for *The Jellyfish Beach Journal*."

I entered a bedroom with posters and toys that indicated it was the boy's. On the far wall, dangerously close to the bed, was a wide circle of destroyed drywall peppered with tiny holes from shotgun pellets.

On the floor beneath the damage was a crumpled pair of wings that looked more like those of a giant butterfly than a bat. At first, I thought the sprite might have escaped, losing only her wings. But nearby, beneath the nightstand, was the corpse.

The deceased sprite had a humanoid body about a foot and a half tall. Her head was disproportionally large, but she was nevertheless beautiful, even with her wounds. The hair in the center of her head, from forehead to neck, stood straight up like a Mohawk haircut—hence the word "crested" in the species' name.

The poor thing must have crawled under the nightstand before dying, which was fortunate, because the father and the police officer apparently hadn't seen her.

I took photos of her and the wall. Then, carefully, I gathered her body and placed it in the shopping bag that had previously held my to-go box from the restaurant. I added the gossamer wings.

As I left the bedroom, the father and Matt were shouting at each other in the living room.

"You have no right to judge me, you little commie!" the man shouted in Matt's face. Matt flinched from the spittle and booze-breath that flew at him.

"I know all about you," Matt shouted back. "You've been arrested for firearm violations before. And you've been busted for fishing and crabbing out of season. What kind of father would fire a shotgun when his child was in his bed only feet away? The state should take your child away from you."

The drunken father lurched toward Matt and was about to take a swing when the officer stepped in between them. She deftly seized the punching arm and got him into some kind of hold.

"You desist right now or I'm taking you to jail!" she shouted at him.

The man went limp. He was outclassed and in the wrong.

"I'll know all about you, too," the man said to Matt with a sneer. "This is a small town. I know now where you work, and I'll find out where you live. I'll be coming for you."

"Rosen, you and your FWC friend need to get out of here to deescalate this situation."

Matt nodded, and I ushered him to the front door, eager to leave.

"Wait, ma'am, what do you have in that bag?"

"A dead bat that might have rabies," I replied. "You can have it after we test it."

"Um, I don't want to get in trouble losing evidence, in case we charge this guy with something."

"I didn't do nothing," he grumbled.

"All the evidence you need is the hole in the drywall," I said.

"Give me your name and number, just in case."

I obliged, and then we left.

"Why did you let that guy get under your skin so much?" I asked Matt, as he drove us away from the house.

"He's a drunken idiot."

"There seemed more to it than that."

Matt was silent for a long while. I glanced at him, the light from the streetlamps we passed streaking across his face, and didn't think he was going to answer. Finally, he did.

"Kids shouldn't die from guns. Period. Aside from the mass shootings, I've always felt a lot of sympathy for those kids you hear about who are killed on the street or in their homes from random gunfire. Not from some twisted sickos, but from careless idiots."

"Like the guy tonight."

"Right."

He went silent again, and I had the instinct not to speak, in case he had something else to say. He did.

"Remember, I told you my younger brother died when he was young? I never said exactly how."

"Was he shot?"

"Yeah. We grew up around here, where we don't have to worry about violent gangs. Nope, just about drunken morons with guns. It was on New Year's Eve, at a backyard barbecue a neighbor had with tons of people. At midnight, we kids set off firecrackers. But some of the adults fired their guns into the sky. Stupid, stupid thing to do. You know how gravity works. What goes up must come down."

"Oh no," I whispered.

"Yeah. Jimmy was hit by a bullet in the top of his head. He lasted in the hospital for four days before he passed."

"I'm so sorry," I said. I squeezed his arm and kissed his cheek.

"Sorry to ruin our date night."

"You didn't ruin it! The Society did."

"No, that drunken bonehead with the shotgun did."

WHEN MATT DROPPED me off at home, my Society handlers were waiting on my front porch.

"Do you have the specimen in that bag?" Mr. Lopez asked.

"I do."

"Good. You always seem to forget to photograph the cryptids you encounter."

"I have the body, and I took pictures of the scene, too."

"Excellent."

"What kind of weapon was used?" Mrs. Lupis asked.

"A shotgun. I hate to say it, but if you wanted to take down a flying sprite, that's probably the best gun choice."

My handlers frowned. Even they realized my words had been in poor taste.

"We'll inform you of the results of the necropsy."

"Thank you. But I was wondering why you've never examined a sprite before."

"They play hard to get," Mr. Lopez said.

"Sprites are extremely shy," said his partner, "and have the ability to fool your senses so you can't see or hear them if they don't want you to. It's a pity that this one let her guard down."

"But what *are* they?"

"The sprite species is part of the Nymph genus and the Fae family," Mr. Lopez said. "But you knew that."

"Of course," I lied.

"In folklore, they're described similarly to elves and

faeries," Mrs. Lupis added. "But sprites don't come into contact with humans as much as those other species. Sprites are much more attached to nature—such as water sprites and meadow sprites—or to the elements. Crested mouth sprites are an exception, because of their need for human teeth."

"I see."

"It took the Society decades before we realized that they're the basis for the tooth-fairy legend."

"What do they do with the teeth they take?"

"They don't actually take them anymore, since parents do that nowadays, and kids want to be paid in the local currency."

"They *handle* the teeth before the human parents show up to take them," Mr. Lopez added. "We're not entirely sure why the sprites do this, except that it involves harvesting energy for their innate magic. It's too bad this sprite didn't use her magic to protect herself. I suppose crested mouth sprites don't normally get attacked by parents. Especially not with shotguns."

With the Friends of Cryptids Society, I learned something new every day.

I went to bed mourning the little creature I had removed from the child's bedroom. And I dreamed of it flying above the suburbs with its colorful butterfly wings. Gunfire erupted from a backyard far below, but the sprite's magic kept it safe.

My dream was happy but was interrupted by my phone ringing.

"Someone just shot up my house!" Matt said breathlessly.

"Are you serious?"

"Yeah. They shot through my bedroom and living room windows, then burned rubber out of here. I'll bet you anything it was the father we saw tonight. Jerome Puttle. I *know* it was him."

"Did you see the car?"

"No. I was afraid to stand up. I could have been killed!"

"Did you call the police?"

"Of course I called the police! They're on the way. But they're not going to be able to catch the guy unless they can enhance the video from my doorbell camera. You can see the car go by, but you can't really make out the license plate. Still, I know it was Puttle."

"Don't do anything rash."

"Since when do I act rashly?"

"All the time."

"Okay, Missy, I'll be very careful and deliberate. But I'm going to make sure that idiot never endangers anyone again."

Matt had his skills and platform as a journalist to get revenge on Puttle, if he kept a grudge against him. The power of the press was Matt's weapon of choice.

I KEPT an eye on him for the next few days, not wanting him to do any of the hotheaded things he could have in response to the drive-by shooting. All seemed quiet until last night when the local news ran a story about a crabber who had been reported missing. Park authorities reported his boat trailer had been left overnight near the Port Inferno boat ramp, which not only wasn't allowed, but meant he'd not returned after a day on the water. Authorities found his boat anchored near the inlet with no one aboard. It was assumed he fell overboard, and a massive search operation took place.

In a panicked text from Matt this morning, he told me it wasn't until someone thought to check on the man's submerged crab traps that they found the body crammed inside a trap near his boat.

The man was Jerome Puttle.

CHAPTER 2
CRAB TRAPPED

"I don't know how the heck they squeezed him into the trap," said a toothless old man at the boat ramp to no one in particular.

The ramp was busy with first responders, the media, and curious onlookers. Matt paced back and forth nervously while the medical examiner's team wheeled the crab trap covered with a tarp into the back of a van.

"They can't get him out," the old man continued. He had noticed that I was listening to him, so he seized upon me to be his audience. "They're gonna have to cut through the wire."

I assumed the trap was like the others stacked on the deck at the stern of the boat, which was tied up at the ramp's pier and cordoned off with yellow crime-scene tape. The traps were rectangular and made of heavy wire mesh, with an opening on one end and a bait basket in the middle.

It did look rather improbable that a man could fit inside the trap, but according to the authorities, he had.

"See that guy pacing back and forth like he has to go to the bathroom?" the old man asked, pointing at Matt. "He was on a paddleboard next to the empty boat when it was anchored out yonder."

I nodded, not mentioning that I knew him.

"I was collecting my own traps nearby and motored over," the man continued. "The guy asked me if I'd seen the owner of the boat. I told him it belongs to Jerome Puttle, who always raids my traps. I noticed one of Puttle's buoys floating among mine, in my territory, so I went to pull up the trap. Too heavy. Thought it was snagged on the bottom, so I asked the nervous guy to help me. He got on my boat, we pulled on the rope, and finally got the trap to the surface. Puttle was inside."

This did not look good for Matt. The officer at Puttle's home the other night had witnessed Matt arguing with Puttle. Then, Matt made a police report blaming Puttle for shooting at his bungalow. What was Matt doing paddleboarding to the victim's boat? I walked over to him and joined his pacing.

"This does not look good for me," he said.

"You think? Why were you at his boat?"

"I didn't know it was his. I was just fishing from my paddle-board this morning. I come here often because the fishing's good, and it's a nice park with easy access to the water. When I saw the unoccupied boat anchored in a busy traffic area, I remembered reports about a fisherman who'd gone missing, so I paddled over to take a look."

"Look, my two favorite people," said a woman behind us.

It was Detective Cindy Shortle, the smarter of the department's two detectives, but the least experienced.

"Mr. Rosen, how convenient for you to remain at the crime scene."

"What do you mean?" The blood draining from his face told me he knew exactly what she meant.

"Officer Bird was telling me about you." She pointed to the cop from the other night who was now speaking with a civilian on the opposite side of the ramp. "She said you knew the victim."

"I've reported on some of his brushes with the law. And I was there on the night he fired a shotgun in his kid's bedroom."

"You had some heated words with him."

"Yeah. I was angry that he had been so reckless."

"And you reported shots were fired at your bungalow."

"Not 'at.' They were fired *into* my place."

"You claimed Mr. Puttle did it."

"Yeah. Wouldn't you think he did it after our 'heated words'? Besides, I did some research, and he owns a car that looks like the model seen on my doorbell camera. I gave the video to you guys."

"Why were you here this morning? Isn't this a bit off your home turf?"

"I frequently paddleboard here. Launching is easy next to the ramp, and the fishing is awesome." He gave her the same story he had told me.

"I see." She turned away as someone at the ramp attracted her attention. "Don't leave town, Rosen. We might need to chat a little more."

"This does not look good for me," Matt said to me again after Shortle had left. "Out on the water, there are no surveillance cameras. All I have is my word that I had nothing to do with killing Puttle."

"How did he die? Was he shot before he was put in the crab trap?"

"From what I overheard from the first responders, he drowned. Someone stuffed him into the trap while he was alive."

"No offense, but you don't seem strong enough to stuff a large man into a crab trap . . . but you're still strong enough to be attractive," I added quickly.

Matt sighed. "I don't believe the police will factor in my strength or lack thereof."

"Maybe you should get a lawyer. Just in case."

"Yeah. I can talk to the newspaper's attorney. She won't be able to help me with my situation, but she can refer me to someone."

"I know an excellent attorney."

"I don't want a werewolf for an attorney."

"Paul is good," I said defensively. "Who cares about his lycanthropy? As we've learned, tons of successful business owners in this town are werewolves."

"I'll think about it," he grumbled, engrossed in his worries.

"You'll be fine. A guy like Jerome Puttle would've had a lot of enemies. I'm sure a more likely suspect will turn up."

I SHOULD HAVE KNOWN that I would end up involved in finding said suspect, and that I would be steered toward finding one who wasn't human.

"You really think it was a revenge killing?" I asked Mrs. Lupis and Mr. Lopez, who had turned up in their matching gray suits at my front door unexpectedly that evening, as they so often did.

"It could be," replied Mr. Lopez. "We know little about crested mouth sprites, but the Fae family of creatures can be quite violent, as you know."

"We believe they have some sort of governing structure, even if it's simply clan leaders," Mrs. Lupis said. "Another sprite will be allowed to take over the territory of the dead one. After all, children will continue to lose their baby teeth."

"That's where you come in," her partner said. "You need to make contact with the new sprite around here."

"And do what?" I asked, though I feared the answer.

"Find out if he or she killed this human. Or knows who did."

"He or she? I thought tooth fairies were female."

"They can be of either gender," said Mrs. Lupis. "This species is involved only in dental matters, and the males have to work, too."

"How am I supposed to find a crested mouth sprite?"

Mr. Lopez looked at me like he thought I was joking.

"Follow the teeth," he said. "What else? Some crested mouth sprites are believed to visit dentist offices, but the best way to find one is to follow the ancient tradition of placing fallen baby teeth under pillows."

"Well, you make it sound so easy that I have to ask why you guys haven't found more mouth sprites."

"It's not so easy. That's why we need you."

"We already told you sprites can trick humans' eyesight to

make themselves invisible," Mrs. Lupis explained. "As a witch, though, you can block their magic."

"And block the sprite from sensing you," added Mr. Lopez. "Do you know any children who just lost a tooth?"

"Um, no."

"Well, find one. Soon."

"Kids don't drop teeth every day like hens lay eggs, you know."

"I suggest, then, that you carry a pair of pliers."

My two handlers showed themselves to the door without so much as a goodbye.

Being childless myself, and in my forties, I didn't exactly hang out with young mothers. Nor did I spend time on mommy social media. In fact, not being part of a large family meant I didn't have nieces or nephews.

And to be perfectly honest, being a witch who worked in a botanica and as a part-time nurse for vampires and were-wolves, I wasn't the kind of person you'd want your young children to be around.

But my business partner, Luisa, had a large extended family. I was pretty sure she had nieces and nephews who were of tooth-shedding age. I asked her about them at work the next day.

"Jorge lost a tooth last week," she told me.

I perked up. "That's excellent! When is the next one coming out?"

"How should I know? I'll ask my sister."

"If he has any that are beginning to come loose, can you ask her to speed up the process?"

"What are you talking about? You want her to pull her son's tooth?"

"No. Just maybe wiggle it a bit now and then. Do we sell any potions that make teeth fall out?"

"No, we don't. I don't know about those nuts at the Society," Luisa said. "They're becoming more and more unreasonable."

The bell above the door rang, and in came Madame Tibodet with her zombie brother, Carl.

Another reason I don't know many kids: who wants to bring their children to a store where a zombie wanders around?

"How can I help you, my dear?" Luisa asked the voodoo priestess.

"I need another box of dried chicken feet," she replied in her melodic Caribbean accent. "I've been going through them so quickly lately. The loas are very demanding."

"Do you have any magic that loosens teeth?" I asked her.

"You know I am a priestess, not a sorceress," she said, frowning.

Carl moaned. He had been reanimated against his will by a sorcerer, so he wasn't a big fan of the profession.

"My apologies," I said.

After the pair left the botanica, I made Luisa promise me she'd alert me the moment Jorge lost a tooth.

"You need to check in with your sister regularly," I said. "Boys like to play rough, and a tooth could be knocked out with no warning."

"Got it."

Luisa stared at me like I was a ghoul.

MATT HOSTED me at his bungalow for dinner as a make-good for our interrupted date the other night. Of course, the setting wasn't quite as elegant, to put it mildly. His 1920s-era home showed its age, partly because his furniture was almost as old as the structure. Overall, the building appeared to be a Category Two hurricane away from becoming kindling wood.

The food was good, but not award-winning like the restaurant's. Matt grilled fresh tuna steaks on his tiny backyard charcoal grill while he drank beer, and I sipped wine.

The atmosphere also wasn't as enchanting tonight as it had been before. Matt was too edgy, as he worried about being a suspect in Puttle's murder.

"Even if Lupis and Lopez are correct, and another sprite killed Puttle for revenge, we need to find a human suspect," he said as he watched over the grill. "Obviously, the police can't pin the murder on a folkloric creature."

"So, you want an innocent person to get arrested?"

"I'm just concerned about *this* innocent person staying free." He pointed the spatula at himself. "Puttle could have been involved in drug smuggling, and no one in that world has perfectly clean hands."

"We've been down this road before with another fisherman," I said, referring to the commercial fisherman, Raul Rivas, who had run drugs from offshore ships to shore.

"Think of Puttle as a low-rent version of Rivas. Maybe we should go speak to our favorite drug lord, Mr. Carrascal."

"I'd rather not. We've also been down the road of environmental extremists, but none of the ones around here have hurt anyone."

Matt slid his spatula beneath the tuna steaks and placed them on a platter. Nicely seared on the outside, and, hopefully, rare on the inside.

"Crabs could be our salvation."

"The tuna will be plenty for me."

"I mean, crabbers might be behind the murder. It sounded like Puttle was poaching someone else's crab traps. Those guys are really protective of their crabs."

I thought of the toothless guy at the boat ramp. "It seems reasonable."

"There's not a huge crabbing industry around here, unlike other parts of Florida, which would make the competition even more ruthless."

"We'll look into it," I said, eyeing the steaks on the platter. "But let's eat first."

Even here, behind the bungalow, we could hear the banging on Matt's front door.

"I wonder who that could be?" I mused.

Matt went pale. "Hopefully, just a Jehovah's Witness."

But when we went inside and opened the door, we found Detective Shortle and Officer Bird.

"Hello, friends!" Shortle said, with fake exuberance. "Got a minute, Rosen?"

"We were just about to eat," he said. Holding the platter of tuna added credibility.

"I just want to ask you a few questions."

"Let me guess. About Puttle's death?"

"See? We're on the exact same page. I tell you what, why don't you be my guest at the station while we talk?"

"Right here is fine."

"Ah, Rosen, it's just not the same as our cozy interview room."

"Yeah, my place isn't wired to record audio and video of our conversation."

"There you go, on the same page again. What do you say? You won't be gone long, and I'll bring you right back here."

"Am I under arrest?"

"You would know it if you were under arrest. This is just a voluntary interview."

"Meaning I don't have to volunteer to go?"

"Yes, but that puts you in a terrible light."

"I think I should get a lawyer."

"That would make this casual conversation awkward, wouldn't it? You realize that if you come with me, you're free to go at any point?"

"Okay, okay, I'll go so I can prove to you I wasn't involved in this crime. And this will be brief, I can assure you." He turned to me. "Missy, please eat without me. I'll join you shortly."

"I can call Paul for you."

"Not tonight. I'm fine." He leaned over to whisper in my ear. "Don't worry, I won't say anything stupid."

I watched him get into the back of a patrol car before it backed down the cobblestone driveway to the street. An hour went by before he called me.

"Can you please pick me up at the station? I walked out of

the interview, and it appears that Shortle's promise of a ride home wasn't sincere."

During the quick trip to the station, I called Paul Leclerc and left a message that we would almost certainly need his services. Right away.

CHAPTER 3
CRESTED MOUTH SPRITE

Not every mother would allow a witch to hide in her young son's closet while he slept. Fortunately, Jorge's mother, Lidia, was accustomed to her older sister's strange profession as a Santeria priestess who ran a botanica with a witch for a partner. She knew what she was in for when she told her sister that Jorge had just lost another tooth.

Even luckier, Lidia's husband was a long-haul trucker who was out of town and wouldn't barge into the bedroom with a shotgun.

Jorge thought it was cool for the strange lady to hide in his closet, and I had to keep reminding him to go to sleep and to stop making funny sounds to make me laugh.

The crested mouth sprite—aka the tooth fairy—would use magic when she arrived to ensure the boy was asleep. She would also direct her magic at me once she discovered I was here, so I cast a protection spell around myself. The spell would also prevent the sprite from sensing my presence before I came out of hiding.

I didn't have to wait long in the closet stuffed with toys and outgrown clothing. Crested mouth sprites know that parents perform the teeth-for-money switcheroo before they retire for the evening, so the sprites must get to work shortly after the child is put to bed.

I got goosebumps along my arms the moment the sprite appeared in the bedroom. I saw her materialize as I gazed through the slightly open closet door.

Yep, it was a female, and she looked like what you'd expect in a tooth fairy. Unlike the carcass I had collected in the shotgun incident, the creature was manifesting as a beautiful, delicate waif on dragonfly wings. She looked quite a bit like Tinker Bell.

She flew above Jorge's head and hovered there while a surge of magic emanated from her, setting off additional goosebumps on my scalp. Jorge's breathing became deep and steady.

The sprite dropped to his bed, rummaged beneath the pillow, and pulled out a central incisor. The tooth looked giant in her tiny hands. She gazed at it like it was the Holy Grail, and I sensed an increase of elemental energy in the air.

The tooth glowed, and so did the sprite. My witchy nature allowed me to feel the power, that she was harvesting from the tooth, growing within her. The sprite even increased in size.

I discreetly opened the closet door a bit and took photos with my phone. The Society gets mad when I forget to photo-graph cryptids.

The sprite returned the tooth beneath the pillow and

flapped her wings, hovering once more above Jorge's sleeping head, looking down upon him fondly.

I took more pictures.

Suddenly, the sprite disappeared.

Just as I was opening the closet door, it slammed shut in my face. Someone was in the closet with me.

I shined my phone's flashlight to reveal a woman looming over me, her head poking out between little-boy shirts on hangers.

"Why are you spying on me?" she asked in a hoarse whisper.

The sprite had taken on a human form, as the species of the Fae family often do, and it was a frightening one. She was large and muscular, with the face of an old crone. Her fingernails were black and inches long. Primitive tattoos were etched on her face and forehead. The chlorine-like smell of ozone wafted from her and made me claustrophobic in this small space.

It took a moment for my hyperventilating to slow enough for me to speak. I had to remind myself that I was safe thanks to my protection spell.

"Oh, hello. My name is Missy Mindle. I represent the Friends of Cryptids Society of the Americas. What's your name?"

"Rachel."

"Pretty name, but not what I'd expect for a sprite."

"What is a cryptid?" She had an accent I couldn't quite place. I would have expected a tooth fairy to have an English accent, because that's the universal storybook narrator's accent here in America. But she sounded more like a tough girl from Chicago.

"Cryptids are legendary creatures that some people are certain exist, though there is no scientific proof. They include sprites, such as yourself, and various monsters and other supernatural creatures. Our Society catalogs, studies, and protects all of you."

"Protect me? Ha! What do you really want with me?" she asked antagonistically.

"Only to prove that you exist. Everyone thinks the tooth fairy is just folklore, but here you are. In the flesh, in a manner of speaking."

"Yeah. I'm here all right. Very observant of you. Back in the old days, we used to take the teeth, but now we must leave them for the parents. They just throw them away, which is a total waste."

"So, you harvest the energy from the teeth to add to your innate magic, right?"

"You're not as dumb as you look. The baby teeth of children are full of rare energy that we need to feed our magic."

I had turned off my flashlight so as not to be rude, but I could see the crone's face studying the contents of the closet.

"American families spend so much money on crap for their kids," the sprite said. "Look at all these toys licensed from movie franchises. The boy doesn't even play with them anymore."

"Oh, you know a lot about our culture?"

"I don't just harvest energy. I observe as a critic of human society, you could say. It's the fun part of my job, getting a glimpse into human lives."

"Really?"

"Yeah. This boy has an older sister who's off gallivanting with a bad-news boyfriend. His father is a trucker who's halfway across the country, and the mother is waiting in the hallway for you to leave her son's bedroom. Overall, a normal, decent family."

"Unlike others?"

"You wouldn't believe the stuff I see in the secret lives of families. I guess you could say I'm nosy. But I get extra energy from prying into private lives."

"In that case, you can't fairly judge me for spying on you," I said.

She frowned, then laughed. "I guess you're right."

"Did you hear about the sprite who was, um, killed?"

"That's why I'm here. I'm taking over her territory."

"Do you know who killed the man who murdered her?"

"No. Like I said, I'm new. I've never been in this territory before. But that man got what was coming to him. You humans may have overrun the earth, but you're all beasts, you are. I can't believe all the despicable, scandalous things I've seen behind the closed doors of your homes. You say you study monsters, but maybe you should take a closer look at your-selves. You're the true monsters."

"You're making me believe you killed the man." I smiled to take the edge out of my accusation.

It didn't work. "I did *not* kill him. Sprites don't kill humans," she said with anger. "If your silly Society was legiti-mate, you'd know a sprite didn't do it."

"Your species is difficult to study. My colleagues at the Friends of Cryptids Society would love to meet you."

They hadn't yet ordered me to capture the sprite, but I was

afraid they would, eventually. If I could only get her to pay a visit to their laboratory . . .

"Missy, who are you talking to in there?" Lidia whispered from the other side of the closet door. "Is the tooth fairy in there?"

The crone disappeared from the closet. I emerged to find Lidia checking under Jorge's pillow while he still slept. She removed the tooth and replaced it with cash.

We tiptoed from the room, and, as soon as Lidia closed the door, she asked me, "Did you see her?"

"Yeah. In some ways, she's like the tooth fairy of legend. In others, she's like your obnoxious neighbor who gets into your business."

Lidia's face filled with confusion.

"Don't worry," I said, patting her arm. "The tooth fairy is real and harmless. It's nice to know at least one myth from our childhood is actually true."

I RETURNED HOME, surprised that Mrs. Lupis and Mr. Lopez weren't there waiting for me. After pouring a glass of wine, I texted them the photos I had taken of the crested mouth sprite, along with my notes from the meeting. These included her physical description in sprite and human forms, rough weight estimates, and an in-depth account of her drawing energy from the tooth.

I added my observation that the sprite appeared to know nothing about Puttle's death along with her assertion that sprites don't kill humans.

Because Jorge had been put to bed so early, I had time to relax before my bedtime. I poured more wine and picked up the mystery novel I had recently begun.

I hadn't even taken a sip or turned a page when the doorbell rang. I opened the door expecting to find my handlers, but Fred Furman stood there instead.

"Sorry to bother you so late," he said. "I just left a meeting of the Downtown Merchants Association and need to talk to you."

The association members were almost all werewolves. For no reason that I have heard other than coincidence, many of the shops, galleries, and eateries on and near Jellyfish Beach Boulevard were owned by wolf shifters.

"Is this about my mother?" I asked.

"How did you know?"

"She said she was going to rule over you all like a mob boss and demand protection money. I didn't think that would go over very well."

"It hasn't. Everyone is complaining. We got rid of a corrupt city commissioner, and now we have to deal with the same problems from an evil sorceress."

I glanced at the invitation on the living room end table. It was from my mother, demanding that all witches join her coven under the threat of death should one refuse. A magical progress bar printed at the bottom showed my deadline was just around the corner.

"I have my own problems from Ruth," I said.

"That's why I'm here. The witches and werewolves have the same enemy. We should join forces to defeat Ruth and drive her out of town."

"Okay. Not a bad idea. But what do you want from me?"

"You're her daughter."

"Only by birth. She's tried to kill me before and will do it again." I glanced at the card. "Maybe in a week's time."

"We need someone on the inside of her coven. We werewolves are just marks to be exploited. But witches like you belong to her coven. You're behind the enemy lines, as they say."

"I'm not a member."

"But that's what we in the association are requesting. For you to join the coven so you're on the inside."

"Her coven is not a little magic club where they get together, drink tea, and swap spells. It's a cult that worships her. They're all brainwashed and are like her slaves."

"I'm confident you won't be brainwashed."

"Don't be so sure."

"When you're on the inside, you'll know what she's up to. That will help us plan our strategy to defeat her."

"You want a spy. Why don't you just say it?"

"Okay. We want you to be our spy. Who better than her own daughter?"

"You don't understand the relationship I have with her. She would trust me less than her other minions."

Furman looked at me with sad brown eyes that reminded me of my childhood dog when he was begging for a treat.

"She'd kill me if she found out," I added.

"It sounds like she's going to kill you anyway if you don't join. We're only asking you to play along with her wishes while helping to bring about her downfall."

"Well . . ."

"I'm sorry to say that your choices are to join her coven, die, or kill her before she kills you. This way, you'll have all of us werewolves on your team. Between our physical lethality and your magic, we can beat your mother."

"She's more powerful than you can imagine."

"Spoken by someone who's been fighting against her as an army of one. This time, you'll have all of us, along with anyone from the coven you can convince to revolt against her."

He was correct. Ever since she re-emerged . . . okay, dive-bombed back into my life, I've had to deal with her on my own. This town had never had a coven, and I'd always practiced magic alone. It would have been nice to be part of a coven, but not a black-magic cult that worshipped Ruth.

Yet, if we defeated her, her coven could stay together for benevolent purposes.

"All right," I said to Fred. "I'm in. But something tells me she won't make it easy."

CHAPTER 4
CRABBY CRABBER

"Not you two again! Something tells me you're not here to go fishing."

Captain Bill Tendrix glared at us from behind the desk in his tiny office at the Jellyfish Beach Marina. The captain and owner of the Sea Fog charter fishing boat had reluctantly helped us investigate a string of earlier murders.

"I'm afraid we're here to ask you about another dead guy," I said.

"Jerome Puttle? I heard about his demise. Can't say I'll miss him."

"Did he keep his boat at this marina?" Matt asked.

Tendrix snorted derisively. "That lowlife? He couldn't afford the rates here. I think he kept his boat at a storage place and trailered it to the Port Inferno boat ramp every day."

"We'll get right to the point," Matt said. "Who do you think killed him?"

"Who knows? I know nothing about the company he kept."

"Do you think he ran drugs for Carrascal?"

"Nah. I think Carrascal is lying low for now with the Feds watching him. He wouldn't hire the likes of Puttle, anyway."

"We're wondering if a rival fisherman or crabber had a beef with Puttle."

"Could be," Tendrix said. "From what I know, Puttle earned his living from fish, spiny lobsters, and crabs, depending on the season. But he was so small time, I don't know why anyone would kill him out of rivalry."

"What if he was stealing someone else's crabs from their traps?"

"Well, yeah. That would rile you up."

"Who could we speak to? Who might know?" I asked.

"A lot of crabbers live down in Port Inferno," he replied, referring to the nearby town named for regularly burning to the ground when it was settled in the nineteenth century. It turned out their first mayor was a pyromaniac. "Ask around at the marina there or just hang out at the boat ramp at the park and look for someone launching an open boat with the console up in the bow. That's definitely a crabbing boat."

We thanked him and walked along the dock to the parking lot.

"I think we should go to the boat ramp first," I said to Matt, "since Puttle didn't keep his boat in a marina. Maybe we'll run into that old guy who you helped pull out the trap that had Puttle in it."

Matt blanched. "Thanks for bringing back horrible memories. If I hadn't been paddleboarding there that morning, I wouldn't be Shortle's prime suspect."

"She said you're her prime suspect?"

"More or less. My interaction with Puttle in front of the police officer was problematic, but also being on the scene of his death doomed me."

"You're not doomed. Don't be so pessimistic. We'll find a more likely suspect."

"*More* likely? You're saying I'm likely?"

"I know you didn't do it, Matt. But if I were a cop who lacked imagination, I might look your way."

"Gee, thanks a lot."

I elbowed him in his ribs. "I'm just messing with you."

"Please don't."

When we arrived at the boat ramp, no one was around except for a few kids fishing from the small pier. There were plenty of pickup trucks with empty trailers parked there, but all the boats were out for a day of fishing or other entertainment.

"I don't know what time of day crabbers go out," Matt said. "Serious fishermen launch before dawn, so some will probably return soon."

We parked in the shade of a grove of palm trees, opened our windows, and waited. Matt's worried expression ruled out engaging in banter with him, so I remained quiet. So did he. It felt like we were waiting for Hell's ferryman to arrive.

A married couple with young kids arrived and created mayhem while Dad clumsily backed their trailer down the ramp and launched the boat. After they left, things were quiet again.

Then, an old boat appeared, riding low in the water. It was filled with white coolers. The driver sat at the console near the bow.

I recognized the stooped-over old man. It was the toothless guy who had helped retrieve the trap holding Puttle.

"There's your buddy," I said to Matt.

He grimaced.

The old man tied his boat to the dock next to the ramp and headed into the parking lot to get his vehicle. That was when we left the car and intercepted him.

"Need any help unloading?" I asked him.

"I recognize this one," he said, pointing to Matt.

"We need to talk to you about Jerome Puttle," Matt said.

"What about him?" asked the man with skin wrinkled and tanned like leather.

"Who do you think killed him?"

The old man laughed. "You want me to narrow down the list?"

"Your name is Larry, right? I forgot to properly introduce myself the other day. My name is Matt, and this is Missy. I'm a reporter for the local paper, and I'm curious to hear your thoughts."

"Only off the record. Not that any of the guys I suspect did it read the paper, but you never know."

"Fine with me," Matt said.

"Let me get my boat out of the water, and then we'll talk."

Larry drove a beat-up old pickup that was actually in better shape than Matt's. He deftly got his boat onto his trailer and out of the water in no time, parking it in the shade near us.

"I got lots of crabs on ice in these coolers," he explained. "I want to keep them cool and alive."

He had installed PVC pipes in the sides of the coolers for ventilation and seemed highly experienced in his trade.

"You make it sound like Puttle wasn't well liked," Matt said. "But among his enemies, who would go so far as to actually kill him, especially by drowning?"

"Jerome didn't care about rules. He was constantly fined by the FWC for poaching crabs and lobsters out of season and violating size restrictions."

"I know," Matt replied. "I did a story about one of his arrests."

"He also didn't much care about rules of fishing etiquette. If you had a secret honey hole, you'd find Jerome in it. But he also stole crabs from other guys' traps. That's as low as you can go."

"Did he steal from you?"

"I caught him more than once."

"You didn't kill him, did you?"

Larry laughed harshly. "Nope. And now I won't have the pleasure. But if you want to talk about his enemies, no one comes close to Burt Umber. The two of them had a feud going on like the Hatfields and McCoys. Jerome stole from Burt all the time, and Burt retaliated by stealing from Jerome."

"Was there ever any violence?"

"Not that I know of."

"Threats of violence?"

"All the time." Larry gave a toothless smile. "From both of 'em."

"Death threats?"

"Death, dismemberment, skinning alive, you name it."

"I see. Maybe it was just talk?"

"It's mighty serious when you interfere with a man trying to make a living. We don't make much money in this line of work. Every buck counts."

"Where can I find Burt Umber?"

"He only works his traps at night, and it would be foolhardy to approach him while he's doing it if you don't want to get shot. He keeps his crabbing boat at the Port Inferno marina and lives on his houseboat there."

"Which houseboat?"

"It goes by the name, *I've Got Crabs.*"

I turned away. "Charming."

"Oh, I see," Matt said. "Thank you for your help."

Larry got into his truck and towed his boat away. Matt and I looked at each other.

"He sounds like he has an agenda," Matt said. "Do you believe him, or is he just trying to damage his rival?"

"Heck, yeah. He has an agenda. But we need to check out Burt Umber, anyway. How did a violent crabber get a name like that?"

"Hippie parents?"

"Probably. They obviously didn't bring him up right."

THE MARINA at Port Inferno was not like the one at Jellyfish Beach. Ours was rather upscale, featuring charter fishing and diving boats as well as sleek yachts.

This marina was the equivalent of a trailer park. A latticework of rickety finger piers connected a sprawling flotilla of grungy commercial fishing boats, old pleasure boats that no longer saw any pleasure, and dismal houseboats.

At the far end of the marina, in a slip near a mangrove forest, we found *I've Got Crabs.* It floated low in the water with a single-story superstructure topped by a sundeck covered with a blue tarp. Blinds covered all the windows, but the glass was so dirty the blinds weren't necessary.

"Welcome to paradise," Matt said.

A dusty pickup truck filled with damaged crab traps sat in a nearby parking lot. I figured it belonged to Umber.

"Since he works nights, he's probably here," I said. "Shall we?"

We walked onto a dock and followed the pier that led to the houseboat. The pier was canted at a dangerous angle because of loose pilings.

I followed behind Matt, trying not to fall into the water, and preparing my truth spell. I didn't use the spell on just anyone, but I had a feeling that Umber was a bad guy, and I wanted to exonerate Matt as quickly as possible.

We stepped aboard the houseboat and inched along the narrow side deck to a nearby door. Matt knocked.

There was no answer, but a scuffling sound came from inside the cabin.

"Someone's in there," I whispered.

Matt nodded and knocked again.

"Hello?" Matt called out.

Still, no one answered. I thought I heard whispering inside.

Matt gave me a meaningful look. I released my truth spell and began building a spell to unlock the door. When it came to spells, I couldn't multi-task very well.

A click came from the doorknob and then from the deadbolt above it.

I returned to preparing my truth spell as Matt swung the door open.

We stepped into a large space, dimly lit by a battery lantern. In the shadows, I could see a sofa and several chairs.

Plus, about thirty men and women.

"*Hola!*" said a smiling man closest to us.

"What the?" I muttered. The surprise discovery had thrown off my spell casting.

The men and women filled the entire space, sitting on all the furniture and the deck.

"Are you the ones taking us to the city?" asked the smiling man.

"We're just friendly neighbors saying hello to Mr. Umber. What—where are you from?"

"We arrived from Cuba last night. Mr. Umber gave us rides here from the sailboat."

"Uh-huh. And where would Mr. Umber be?"

The telltale slide of a pistol chambering a round came from behind us.

"I'm right here," said an unseen man. "Welcome to my humble abode. Make yourself at home. Before I kill you."

CHAPTER 5
BURT UMBER

The man poked me in the back with the gun and shoved me forward with his other hand. He did the same with Matt. The Cubans moved out of the way, clearing a path for Umber to herd the two of us forward through the boat to the wheelhouse in the bow.

Umber unlocked the door and pushed us inside. He entered behind us and closed the door.

"Who are you, and why are you on my boat?"

"We're your new neighbors," I said with a fake smile.

Umber was a middle-aged man, just as weathered as Larry, but with most of his teeth intact. He had a full head of perfectly coiffed black hair and was well over six muscular feet tall.

I would say he had the strength to stuff a man in a crab trap.

"I'll be honest with you," Matt said. "We're with *The Jelly-fish Beach Journal.*"

He often claimed I was employed by the paper because it

was a simpler explanation when interviewing people than saying I was just a friend and a witch. I believed it also gave me extra security, implying we both had an institution backing us that would seek retribution if we were harmed.

Umber frowned. Okay, I take that back. Maybe saying we worked for the newspaper made it more likely we'd be killed.

"What does that rag want with me?" he demanded.

"We want you to help us find the murderer of Jerome Puttle," Matt said.

Umber spat on the deck. "Who cares about that loser? He stole from other crabbers and poached lobsters and crabs out of season. I heard he even fired a shotgun in his kid's bedroom."

"That, he did," I said.

Meanwhile, I cast a protection spell around Matt and me. It was strong enough to keep Umber away from us, and I kept feeding it energy to make it strong enough to stop a bullet.

"Did you kill Puttle?" Matt asked.

Umber snorted. "Yeah, as if I would tell you."

"Did someone else kill him?"

"You're a stupid little pipsqueak. Rule Number One: don't ask the guy aiming a gun at you if he killed someone."

"I'm giving you the opportunity to clear your name."

"Clear it from what? You got nothing connecting me to Puttle's death. Which could have been accidental, by the way."

"It wasn't accidental. He didn't crawl into that crab trap by himself. And we've spoken to people who claim you two were feuding."

"If you call objecting to someone stealing from you *feuding*, then yes."

He glanced behind him as low conversations came from the main salon. When he turned back to us, his face was grim.

"You shouldn't have come here and seen them. I can't allow you to tell anyone about them, but I don't want them to hear what I'm going to do to you. You're going to stay here until their rides get here, then we're going for a nice boat trip."

And experience the fate of Jerome Puttle, I thought.

"Give me your phones," Umber ordered.

"No," I said, confident that my protection spell was bullet proof.

Umber reached toward my back pocket. Until his hand hit the protection bubble.

"What happened?" he asked.

Maintaining the protection spell, I worked on a sleep spell to take Umber out. Most of my elemental energies had gone into the protection spell, but I should have enough left over to put the man to sleep.

Suddenly, Matt poked his arms from his protective bubble and shoved Umber, knocking him off balance. As Umber careened toward the wall, Matt tried to grab his gun. Umber yanked the gun away, and Matt seized Umber's arm with both hands.

The good thing about my protection spell was that you could exert force out from it. Nothing should be able to enter the bubble except, perhaps, a bullet.

Umber fired. The gunshot hurt my ears in the confined wheelhouse, but I could hear the bullet slam into the wall after ricocheting off the protection bubble.

A woman squealed in the salon. Umber pushed against

Matt's bubble and slammed him against the wall, trying to break free of him.

My concentration on the sleep spell was broken. So, I moved toward Umber. His hand that held the gun was still trapped in Matt's grip, so I kicked it. The firearm flew free, clattering to the deck in the corner.

Umber scrambled to retrieve it, then fled the wheelhouse. A few seconds later, a truck engine rumbled to life outside.

"That man is going down for this," I said.

"I'm going to report him to Shortle right now," said Matt. "I guess I need to report the Cubans, too."

However, when we left the wheelhouse, we found the houseboat deserted. All the migrants had fled, probably scattering throughout the area toward Miami, where there was little chance they would be found by immigration authorities.

We waited on the upper deck of the houseboat and waved Shortle over when we saw her car arrive at the marina. We met her down in the salon.

When she entered, she took great interest in the empty water bottles and snack wrappers left on the deck.

"How many migrants were there?" she asked.

"I counted twenty-seven," Matt said.

"I already notified ICE. They said this wasn't the first time migrants were ferried to shore around here."

"It looks like this was Umber's side hustle," Matt said. "He probably needed extra income with Jerome Puttle stealing his crabs all the time."

"Okay, now this all makes sense," Shortle said. "You're trying to pin Puttle's death on this guy. Burt Umber is his name?"

"Yes, and we're not trying to pin anything on anyone. We heard that there was a feud between him and the victim. It sounded like Umber had a believable motive for getting rid of him."

"We'll see about that," Shortle said with skepticism. "You're not out of the woods yet, Rosen."

"Aww, come on. You like me. You know I didn't do it."

"That's a negative on both of those assertions."

"Whether he killed Puttle or not, Umber has to be arrested," I said. "He's not just a human smuggler. He was going to kill us."

"I know. Rosen told me over the phone. But you two action heroes disarmed him."

"Yes, we did. Temporarily."

"Bravo. Not bad for a guy who takes notes at city council meetings and a witch who works in a bodega."

"Botanica. And I'm not a real witch. Just a hobbyist."

"Yeah, right. Anyway, when we find Umber, we'll interrogate him about Jerome Puttle. Does that make you happy?"

"Somewhat. You should have talked to him about that already. It wasn't hard to find out about the feud between them. But no, you were so certain I was the murderer."

"It's too early to say I'm certain, Rosen. Okay? But some others in the department are. And they're gonna keep their eyes on you, so you'd better avoid doing anything stupid."

"Since when have I done anything stupid?" Matt asked. But his face darkened when he was flooded with all the memories of him doing so. "Never mind."

"You guys go home," Shortle said. "I'll wait here for ICE to arrive."

We got into Matt's truck and headed back toward nearby Jellyfish Beach.

"I consider today a success," I said.

"What do you mean? Umber got away."

"We didn't need to catch him. I wasn't assigned to solve Puttle's murder. All we needed to do was make the police consider someone other than you as their prime suspect. We told Shortle about the feud between him and Umber, and now they're going to arrest Umber for smuggling the migrants and assaulting us."

"Yeah. I guess you're right. But I won't feel better until I'm totally in the clear."

"I understand. But please try to chill out."

"What if Umber didn't kill Puttle?"

"I'm sure he did."

"But what if he didn't?"

I sighed. "We'll have to start again at square one."

Matt brooded silently for the rest of the drive, which wasn't long. As we headed down Jellyfish Beach Boulevard, a police cruiser passed us, lights flashing, headed toward the beach. Seconds later, another one passed us. Then came a third.

It was practically half our police department.

"We're just a block from my place," Matt said. "Do you mind if I run inside and listen to the police scanner?"

"No, go ahead. It goes with your job."

I wished he would just take me home, but throughout its history, Jellyfish Beach has experienced very little crime, and Matt was dying of curiosity. I could always walk home from there if he got wrapped up in something big.

45

"It's probably just a dangerous traffic stop," Matt said, parking the truck in front of his bungalow.

I followed him into his living room where he kept the scanner on a side table. He turned on the unit that looked like a radio receiver with a telescoping antenna.

"Dispatch, this is Unit Three," said a male voice with background static. "I've arrived at the scene of the reported Code Five, at ten-sixty-six Ocean Drive. Requested the property manager to unlock the unit's door. She said she's the one who called nine-one-one."

"Ten-four. Keep us updated."

"Okay, I'm going in now . . . Oh, man! Golly, I think I'm going to be sick."

"Jenkins, what is it?"

"There's a male victim. Deceased. On the living room floor."

"How do you know he's deceased?" the dispatcher asked.

"Let me put it this way: he's been deceased for days. I've got to open some windows."

"This is Unit Two. I've arrived on the scene."

"No need to hurry inside," Jenkins said. "We need crime-scene investigators here. And the medical examiner."

"They're on the way. So is Detective Glasbag. Let's have radio silence unless there's a critical need," said the dispatcher.

"They know people like me listen to them," Matt explained. "That's why the dispatcher asked for radio silence. I want to go to the scene to learn more before any of the other news media show up."

I looked at him dubiously. What other news media? *The Jellyfish Beach Journal* was the only game in town, the nearest TV and radio stations being a half hour away. I mentioned this.

"Well, whoever's assigned to the city desk this afternoon at *The Journal* will take this story. I want to beat him or her to it."

"Why?"

"Because it's a big story! There's rarely a murder in Jellyfish Beach."

"Since we started working together, there have been many."

"Just a coincidence. Anyway, the story will get picked up by the wire services and the broadcast outfits. I want it to be my story."

"Then, let's go there now."

He hesitated. "I'll drive you home first."

"No, I don't mind going with you."

"It'll just take a few extra minutes. I'll drop you off on my way to the crime scene."

"Absolutely not. I'm going with you."

"It sounds like it's a ghastly scene."

"They won't let me get close to it, anyway. Stop messing around, and let's go."

Matt sighed with exasperation when we walked outside to his truck. I couldn't understand why he was suddenly being so protective of me. After all, I'd been to many crime scenes with him. It was almost like a couple's activity for us.

We drove across the Intracoastal bridge onto the barrier island and headed north to the address we had heard on the police radio. It was an older condo, nothing fancy. It was similar in age and architecture to Squid Tower, where the retired vampires lived.

Matt flashed his reporter's badge to a guard to get through the entrance gate, and we parked in a visitors' lot near three patrol cars and an ambulance that wouldn't be needed.

The front doors of the condo units were on exterior breezeways, and we easily spotted the unit in question by the police officers milling about its open door on the second floor.

"You stay here," Matt told me, pulling his reporter's notebook from his back pocket. "I'll be back soon."

Stay here? Did he think I was a kid or a dog? I waited a few seconds after he walked away, then followed him at a distance. I took the stairs and exited on the second-floor breezeway.

Matt was speaking with two officers outside the open door of the condo. He craned his neck to see inside, but they wouldn't let him enter. They were shielding his tender eyes just like he had tried to do with me.

"The crime-scene tech is guessing the vic has been dead for three days," a young male officer said, "but the medical examiner will be able to tell us a more exact time when she gets here."

"Haven't you had enough of murder scenes, Rosen?" asked the other officer, Bird, the same woman who had been at the tooth-fairy shooting.

"We're all just doing our jobs here," Matt replied. "You said the cause of death was blunt-force trauma?"

"Yeah," the male officer said. "The vic was beaten to death with a Venus de Milo statuette."

"How ironic," Matt commented.

"What do you mean?"

"You said the victim's name is Charles Chubb?" he asked.

"Yeah?"

"If it's the same one I know, he's been arrested several times for spousal abuse," Matt said. "Maybe his wife gave him what he deserved."

"No one deserves that."

"Neither did his wife. Has anyone spoken with her?" Matt asked.

"Not yet. We spoke to a neighbor who said she and the victim were divorced. The detective will try to track her down."

Officer Bird studied Matt, frowning. "This is the second murder victim you knew."

"I didn't really know him," Matt replied. "I reported on him. Asked him a few questions. I cover crime, and this is a small city. So, I know of many of the criminals."

"Takes one to know one," she muttered.

"Excuse me? What are you implying?"

"Nothing at all."

Matt appeared eager for a confrontation, but everyone's attention was diverted when the medical examiner arrived. The woman, in her late fifties, entered the condo and asked questions of the crime-scene techs.

Matt noticed me standing on the breezeway nearby.

"What are you doing here?" he asked.

"Don't treat me like a naughty child. I was simply curious."

"A notorious wife beater was beaten to death. I wonder if the wife did it."

Detective Marty Glasbag emerged from the stairwell and walked toward us.

"Rosen, what a surprise seeing you here."

"What's that supposed to mean?" Matt asked defensively.

"Only that you're always at murder scenes. Like flies around a corpse."

"I have a police scanner."

"I figured. Now, maybe you and your friend should go down to the parking lot. Or, even better, go home. I just got here, so I've got no information to tell you."

"Hey, have you guys tracked down Burt Umber?"

"The migrant smuggler? I don't know. You'll have to ask Detective Shortle."

"Yeah. I'll do that."

"Let's go," I said, leading the way to the stairs.

But when we reached the parking lot, Matt didn't want to leave.

"This is why I offered to take you home," he said. "I need to ask Glasbag questions when he comes down. If I try to call him later, he might not answer."

"Okay, Mr. In-Your-Face."

"You can't be a reporter from the comfort of your desk chair. You have to observe things with your own eyes and ears. Ask questions face to face." He paused. "Do I sound arrogant?"

"A little."

"I'm passionate about what I do. Maybe too passionate. Perhaps, I should direct some of my passion elsewhere," he said, giving me a knowing look.

"Perhaps, you should."

His phone rang, ruining the moment. He answered it.

"Ah, Detective Shortle. Your name just came up in conversation. No, it was regarding Burt Umber . . . Really? He did? He's probably lying. You're going to check on that, right? Yeah, yeah, sorry. Thanks for calling. Yes, I'm still here . . . What, again? Why? Okay, okay. Tomorrow at nine."

He looked crestfallen.

"What did she say?" I asked.

"She had terrible news for me."

CHAPTER 6
UNDER SUSPICION

"They found Burt Umber and took him into custody for the migrant smuggling. But he claimed he has an alibi for when Jerome Puttle was murdered," Matt said. "Umber told the detective his boat was being repaired, and he went down to South Florida to gamble with friends who will back up his story."

"That's frustrating. He seemed like such an obvious suspect."

"Which leaves me as a prime suspect again," Matt said in a resigned voice.

"Don't worry. We'll investigate some more."

"It's in my nature to worry. And Shortle wants me to come in for another interview tomorrow."

"You're taking Paul Leclerc with you this time," I insisted. "Don't talk to Shortle ever again without Paul."

"Yeah, yeah. Whatever."

"I'm serious."

"I know. And you're right. This is how innocent people get charged with crimes. They have friendly little chats with detectives who tell them they don't need an attorney. Then, they get manipulated and bullied and say things that get taken out of context."

"Exactly."

"And Shortle mentioned something that really bothered me. She wants to question me about the articles I wrote about the latest victim, Charles Chubb."

"Why?"

"I don't know. Maybe she thinks I'm a vigilante or something. I report on bad men who do bad things, and then they end up dead."

I laughed nervously. "Talk about jumping to conclusions."

"Yeah. It's utterly ridiculous. But I'm worried."

I TOLD Matt I would buy him and Paul lunch after their interview at the police station. What Matt didn't know was that I was also paying for Paul's time during this early stage. I wasn't wealthy by any means, but I had some savings, thanks to the original grant from the Friends of Cryptids Society.

I assumed we wouldn't need to retain Paul for a criminal defense, just for Shortle's interviews. But if Matt was charged with a crime, it would be a different ball game. I couldn't afford to pay Paul through an entire trial.

Wait, what was I thinking? Why would Matt be charged with a crime?

We met at Billy's Pizza, close to the police station. That was one of the businesses I had discovered were owned by were-wolves, so I assumed Paul would be familiar with the place.

Sure enough, Johnny, the plump, mustachioed owner, came out from behind the counter and gave Paul a hug when he and Matt arrived. Paul was one of those middle-aged men who insists on wearing a ponytail despite a bald spot in the back.

The one time I saw him in wolf form, there was no bald spot. A perk, I guess, of being a lycanthrope.

"Are profits better now that Commissioner Dunot is gone?" Paul asked.

"No," Johnny replied. "There's a new capo in town with her hand out for contributions."

He glanced at me. Did he know Ruth was my mother? Did everyone in town know?

Matt and Paul sat at my table, and we ordered slices and sodas. My two companions looked gloomy.

"How did it go?" I asked.

"Shortle acts like she believes I killed Puttle," Matt said.

"She wasn't antagonistic," Paul added. "But the thrust of her questioning was to trip Matt up and get him to contradict himself."

"My story hasn't changed at all since she first interrogated me. Why would it? She then asked these hypothetical questions, like 'if you saw him on his boat and you wanted to kill him, how would you do it?' Paul shut those down right away."

"That's one way the police browbeat you into a false confession," Paul explained.

"Then, out of nowhere, she asked me questions about the latest victim, Charles Chubb. I said, 'Why are you asking me about him? He has no connection to Puttle?' And she goes, 'The only connection is you. Both men were reprehensible, and you reported on them.'"

"That means nothing," Paul said, chewing pizza. "Both guys probably ate here at some point. Does that mean Johnny killed them?"

"Who did I kill?" Johnny asked from behind the counter.

"No one. I was only making a point."

"The two victims were killed in different ways for different reasons," Matt said. "Obviously, by different people. Why does Shortle have it in for me?"

He seemed to take it personally. Was he attracted to Shortle? Or was she attracted to him? Why was I feeling jealous?

"The Jellyfish Beach Police Department is understaffed, underfunded, and underperforming," Paul said. "They'd rather try to pin the crimes on one guy than go to the trouble of a serious investigation. We might have to do one ourselves. I could hire a private investigator."

"Too expensive. Matt and I have been to this dance before," I said. "We'll look into it ourselves. We've already begun."

Paul arched his bushy eyebrows. "Suit yourself. I'm here to help."

Matt didn't look as confident as I sounded.

I PARKED along the curb across the street from the small apartment building a couple of blocks north of Jellyfish Beach Boulevard. It was an ugly, unremarkable four-story building, probably about twenty years old. But it gave me the creeps.

The only time I'd been inside it was when I'd been abducted by the Knights Simplar and dragged here with my hands zip-tied behind my back and a hood over my head.

I got out of the car, crossed the street, and took a deep breath. Then, I pressed the buzzer for Ruth's apartment on the second floor.

"Leave the food downstairs," said an unfamiliar voice over the intercom. "I'll come down and get it."

"I don't have any food," I replied. "I'm here to join the coven."

"What coven? There's no coven here."

"I'm Missy Mindle, the daughter of Saint Ruthless."

There was a long pause before a buzz came from the lobby door, followed by a loud click of the lock.

"Come upstairs," the voice said. "No weapons."

I didn't own any weapons. Even my magic wasn't very good at hurting people. I didn't say that, though. I just opened the door, went through the lobby, and took the elevator.

The incense struck me the moment I stepped out onto the second floor.

No, it wasn't incense, just a trace of smoke from something burning. Something nasty. It grew stronger as I approached Apartment 2A.

I rang the doorbell, and the door instantly opened inward.

An overweight, middle-aged man wearing a red leotard stood there. He stroked his beard nervously.

"Are you Missy?" he asked.

"Yes. Are you a witch?"

"I was a wizard in Sea Lice Sound until I was invited to join Saint Ruthless's coven."

"'Invited' is too soft a word," I said, showing him my invitation. The magical progress bar on it was only a millimeter away from the "deadline."

He swallowed. "I guess you can say there's a penalty for not accepting her invitation. Well, come in, come in. Her Holiness isn't here right now—I think she's buying scratch-off lottery tickets with a new spell she developed. But you're welcome to wait. You're almost a saint yourself, being her daughter and all."

"On the contrary."

The last time I'd been here, the furniture had been cleared from the living room and acolytes were seated in a circle as if a ceremony had been in progress. Today, it looked like a normal living room. Two spaced-out women, sprawled on the couch, watched a reality TV show.

"Where is everybody?" I asked.

"At their homes, I presume," replied the man in the leotard. He held a wooden spoon in one hand and looked as though he was eager to return to the kitchen. "This is Saint Ruthless's apartment. I am her manservant, Federico."

"Nice meeting you, Federico."

He nodded and gave a strained smile. "She invites coven members here when needed. The coven is too big to fit in here all at once."

"Oh. Good for her, I guess. I know she meets with the Knights Simplar at their own meeting place."

"Exactly."

"What about the werewolves? Do they meet here?"

He visibly shuddered. "No. They don't come here, thank goodness."

"They're perfectly ordinary in human form. They're business owners downtown."

"Technically, they're not members of the inner coven, since they're not witches or wizards. They're more like dues-paying associate members. More like worshippers."

"I think the dues paying is their main purpose," I said.

Federico nodded nervously.

"Saint Ruthless has a deeply rooted presence throughout all of Crab County," he said.

The way Ruth segmented her followers could make it more difficult for me to spy. I would only witness a small part of her operations. Unless I went full bore and wormed my way into her inner circle. It would be difficult, though, for her to trust me enough.

"I need to get back to my recipe," Federico said. "Please make yourself comfortable out here with the sisters," he gestured toward the TV-watchers. "Can I offer you some water?"

"Please," I said.

"Still, sparkling, or infused?"

"Infused with what?"

"Oh, a citrus-essence brainwashing potion."

"Still, please."

I attempted to follow him into the small kitchen, but he blocked me with his body and reached into the fridge. He handed me a plastic bottle of water that lacked a label.

I took it with me to the living room. As I unscrewed the top, movement caught my eye. I peered closely at the water. Was that an insect swimming in there?

Putting on my reading glasses, I finally made out what the creature was. A microscopic-sized piranha.

I left the bottle on a table.

My nerves prevented me from sitting down, so I stood there and watched the TV. It was on a news channel with a talking head insisting that Satan had taken over the US government.

"So, you guys are sisters?" I asked the two young women sitting zombie-like on the couch, staring blankly at the TV. "You don't look anything alike."

They didn't answer.

"Sorry. My question was rude. I guess I'm a bit nervous today."

"We're not siblings," the taller one said. "We were nuns until Saint Ruthless taught us the black arts."

"You don't happen to know a vampire-nun named Mathilda, do you?"

"No."

"Good. And between us, it's not too late to abandon evil and return to the side of good."

The woman turned her head toward me and opened her mouth. She stuck out her tongue at me. It was black and kept extending and extending until it covered the six feet between us.

I dove sideways, and the tongue just missed hitting my face. Then, it retreated into the woman's mouth like a tape measure.

"Okay, maybe it *is* too late for you."

I moved farther from the woman and returned my attention to the television set. But I kept glancing sideways to make sure the tongue wasn't coming for me again.

The front door burst open, and I jumped. It was my mother. Her short black hair had more gray, and her face had more wrinkles, since I'd last seen her.

The zonked-out former nuns suddenly became animated, leaping from the couch and prostrating themselves to their leader on the hardwood floor.

"I won fifteen bucks on the scratch-offs, and I only spent fifty! All thanks to my magic." Ruth cackled with smug satisfaction. "Oh, what brings you here, dearie?" she said to me. "Are you here to attack me?"

"No. I finally decided to join your coven."

"Why is it I don't believe you?"

"Because I have been obnoxiously self-righteous toward you for so long. But now I've seen the light. I mean, the dark."

"That's fantastic! I've always said black magic will take you to the next level of your craft."

"So, can you deactivate my deadline?" I handed her my invitation. "I don't know if it's like an expiring parking meter, but I don't want to drop dead suddenly even though I've accepted the invitation."

She took the card from me and tore it into pieces, dropping them to the floor.

"That's it?" I asked. "Could I have just torn it up myself?"

"If you wanted to drop dead suddenly." She smiled malevolently.

"Okay. I see. So, what's the onboarding procedure for your coven? Do I have to meet with HR? Are there classes or workshops I need to take?"

She stepped over the prostrated ex-nuns and approached

my chair. I would not get on the floor like the nuns unless she knocked me down.

"The first thing you must do is earn my trust," Ruth said in my face, her breath smelling like black licorice. "You will perform a series of tasks to prove yourself. Like the Twelve Labors of Hercules."

"*Twelve?*"

"I haven't decided on how many yet."

"And I can't go around slaying mythical creatures like Hercules did. I've sworn to protect them. You never said I had to break my contract with the Friends of Cryptids Society. If that's the case, I'll have to walk out of here."

"No, wait! No slaying of mythical creatures. These will be other sorts of tasks and tests."

"Remember, I'm not freakishly strong like Hercules. I can't wrestle and capture a bull. Even with my magic."

"Yes, yes, I know. This will be more like a scavenger hunt," Ruth said, searching on her phone, undoubtedly for a list of Hercules's tasks.

"Oh, that sounds like fun."

"It will *not* be fun. I will order you to do something like he did: clean the Augean stables—thousands of pooping cattle in a stable that hadn't been cleaned in over thirty years."

"Mother—I mean Saint Ruth—"

"Saint *Ruthless.*"

"Sorry. I think you're losing the narrative."

Ruth pulled a crumpled pack of cigarettes from her pocket and lit one.

"You stress me out so much," she said. "That's how I know you truly are my daughter. Forget the reference to Hercules. You will do tasks of my choosing—tasks that will be dangerous and arduous."

She flicked ashes from her cigarette upon the heads of the two sisters still prostrated on the floor behind her.

"For the first one," she intoned, puffing out her chest dramatically, "you will kill—"

"I'm not killing anyone or anything."

She let out a big breath like a deflating balloon. "This is why they say not to hire family members. Anyway, I have decided now. You will capture a legendary creature, like a centaur or a griffin, and bring it to me. You don't have to harm it, but you must catch it and bring it here."

It just so happened I knew a centaur, and he owed me a favor.

"Okay. I accept the challenge. I'll bring you a centaur."

"Really?" She was truly surprised.

"Yeah. It seems like an enormous waste of time, when all I wanted to do was fulfill your request and join your coven. But your wish is my command, Saint Ruthless."

Ruth cackled with glee.

"See," she said to the supplicants at her feet. "I'm so power-ful, even my daughter obeys me!"

She flicked more ashes upon them.

I DROVE HOME, bewildered that Ruth hadn't put me through torture, or at least temporarily imprisoned me. I had even hired a cat sitter, just in case. This hadn't turned out at all like that. Perhaps Ruth was going through some issues.

My phone rang. I thought it would be her ordering me to return to the apartment for torture. Instead, it was Matt.

"I hope your morning is free tomorrow," he said.

"Actually, I'm working at the botanica."

"I set up an appointment for you to meet with Elizabeth Chubb."

"And who is she?"

"The wife of the latest victim, Charles Chubb. Elizabeth had filed several protective orders against her husband because of his abuse. You need to talk to her and get a feeling if she was the one who killed him."

"I do? And where will you be?"

"At work. I can't meet with her—are you crazy? Don't you realize how bad the optics would be? I'm suspected of killing her husband."

"Since when?"

"Okay, not *officially* suspected. Yet. But it's obvious that Shortle is headed in that direction."

"But—"

"She's available at ten. I'll ask her to meet you at the botanica."

I mumbled my agreement.

What was wrong with me? Somehow, I'd saddled myself with being both Matt's detective and Ruth's centaur wrangler.

And then, as they say, the Augean poop hit the fan.

CHAPTER 7
LOW ENERGY

I awoke to a piercing whistle in my head from one of my security wards. Sitting up in bed, I cleared my mind of lingering dreams and focused on the energy sent to me by the ward. It wasn't from one that I had created on my property; it came from the botanica.

At the botanica, we didn't have a burglar alarm like most businesses. Those systems notify the police, who, when they arrived at the store, would be less likely to find a human burglar than a wayward supernatural creature attracted to the spiritual energy there like a moth drawn to a lamp.

We couldn't have an innocent pixie or zombie captured by the police, could we? Nope. Luisa and I had to deal with supernatural trespassers ourselves. Well, actually I had to do it since it was my magic that created the alert, though Luisa was available for backup.

The ward wasn't sophisticated enough to tell me what kind of creature had tripped it, but it did indicate that it wasn't an ordinary human or animal. I hoped it was Carl, who occasionally wandered to the botanica, driven by the power of the Orisha statuettes we sold.

I threw on jeans and a clean T-shirt, then jumped in my car.

The drive was short, and I pulled into a parking space in front of the botanica, bathing the building with my headlights. No creatures were visible, but one of the aluminum hurricane shutters we slide down over the windows was damaged.

That pointed toward a strong but less-intelligent creature, like a zombie or troll.

I turned off the lights and cast a protection spell around myself before exiting the car. The tingling on my scalp told me a supernatural creature was still on the premises.

I cast an additional spell that heightened my senses; the powerful flashlight I carried would not be needed for my vision, but to blind the creature if it was hostile. It was one of those heavy, long, cop flashlights, so I could also bonk the monster on the head if I had to.

Beginning at the Good-to-Go to my left, which was also closed at this hour, I circled the building, finding more signs of tampering with the shutters at the end facing the larger parking lot. Then, as I passed the dumpster and searched the building's rear, I found the intruder.

It wasn't a zombie or a troll. It was Rachel, the crested mouth sprite, in her scary human form. She sat on the asphalt, reclining against the concrete-block wall, appearing like someone suffering from a substance abuse disorder.

"Rachel? Are you okay?" I asked.

She shook her head sadly. "I'm weak and stuck in my human body. Maybe it's best I'm in this form, because it will be daytime soon, and we mouth sprites don't like to fly around in the daylight. Hurts our eyes."

"Why are you stuck as a human?"

"I told you—I'm weak. I haven't harvested any tooth energy for a while. This territory is still unfamiliar to me, and I can't seem to find enough kids who are losing their baby teeth."

"This area used to be mainly a place for older folks, but younger families are moving in. Once you know the territory better, you'll find more teeth, I'm sure. But why are you here at our botanica?"

"Children's teeth are inside. I can sense them."

"Really? I didn't know we carried them. They must have been on the shelf a long time."

"They still have energy, though."

"Okay. We'll go inside and get them," I said, helping her to her feet and leading her to the front of the store. "If you don't mind, I'm going to call a couple of friends who would really like to—"

Mrs. Lupis and Mr. Lopez stood by the front door.

"—meet you." I stopped walking, baffled by my handlers' appearance. "Hi. I was just about to call you guys."

"We know," Mr. Lopez said. "We figured we'd save you the effort."

"Thanks. I guess. I'd like you to meet Rachel, our territory's new crested mouth sprite. Rachel, this is Mrs. Lupis and Mr. Lopez, agents for the Friends of Cryptids Society of the Americas."

"We're delighted to meet you," Mrs. Lupis said. "Let's get you inside and put some teeth in your hands."

I had already disabled the other security wards during my drive here, so all that was needed was to unlock and raise the hurricane shutters, then unlock the front door.

I turned on the lights.

"I confess I'm not certain where the teeth would be," I said.

"Somewhere in the back," Rachel said as she leaned on Mrs. Lupis. "I can feel them."

This was the brightest lighting in which I had ever seen the sprite in her human form. Most species of the Fae family are downright gorgeous when they adopt human forms. Rachel was an exception. Her red hair had the eponymous crest which, combined with her pale skin and devilishly large mouth, made her look like a manic punk rocker.

"I have an idea where to look," I said, leading the others in a procession down the main aisle, past shelves of Christian saints and their permutations in the Santeria and voodoo faiths.

Next, we passed a large assortment of potions, contained in everything from tiny glass vials to plastic gallon jugs. We had love potions, luck potions, hair regrowth potions, and a very effective stain remover, to name a few.

Against the back wall were several apothecary chests of different heights, but of a similar design with their rows of tiny drawers. I was in charge of the one on the right, which held herbs, minerals, and other ingredients for witchcraft. The other chests held materials for Santeria and voodoo, with which I was less familiar.

Rachel pointed to the one on the left. Voodoo stuff. I began opening drawers randomly until I discovered a grouping of ones that held pieces of bones. From what creatures, I was afraid to guess.

Below the bones were the tooth drawers. Lots of fangs and molars from unidentified species. When I opened one that held distinctly human-like teeth, Rachel grinned.

I moved out of the way and let her sort through the drawer, plucking out the tiniest teeth. She held them in both hands and closed her eyes as she absorbed the teeth's psychic energy.

These teeth weren't freshly removed like the ones tooth fairies usually handle, but they made up in quantity what they lacked in quality.

Rachel's rejuvenation was rapid and obvious to my human eyes. She stood up straight, full of vigor. Even the crest of her hair stood straighter.

Mrs. Lupis took photos with her phone, and Mr. Lopez scribbled furiously in a notepad.

But then the bells above the door tinkled. Everyone looked at it in horror, worrying about what the customer might see.

It was only Madame Tibodet with Carl in tow, silhouetted by the faint light of dawn. She didn't appear surprised at all when she saw the sprite in human form getting energized.

"Good morning," the voodoo priestess said in her booming Caribbean voice. "I'm glad you're open so early. Do you have any fresh mandrake root today?"

Carl moaned.

"I think that's shameful," Rachel said, handing me the teeth, which she had no more use for. "That woman created a zombie to be her slave. Isn't that illegal? It should be."

"Don't jump to conclusions," I said. "Carl is her brother. He died a natural death, and a sorcerer brought him back as a zombie. She takes care of him as if he were a human with disabilities."

"So sorry," Rachel said. "I'm too quick to judge you humans. I'm hyper-critical by nature and must learn to give lesser species like yours the benefit of the doubt, in spite of myself. Ah, I feel so much better now with this energy. Thank you for your help!"

Rachel shifted to her natural sprite form. She flew around the store, just below the ceiling, like a cross between a flying squirrel and a dragonfly. Madame Tibodet opened the door, and Rachel flew out, disappearing into the sky.

It would have been the perfect happy ending, had her buzzing throughout the store not spooked Carl. The zombie freaked out, to put it mildly.

With a long, anguished moan, he rushed deeper into the aisles, away from the sprite. Even after she had gone, he moaned and thrashed his arms, sending ceramic saints and bottles of potions smashing on the floor.

His sister's cries for him to calm down went unheeded, and he knocked a wire rack holding bags of herbs into a glass case containing incense burners.

Madame Tibodet's chasing him around wasn't helping. Mrs. Lupis and Mr. Lopez stayed out of the way, watching dispassionately like zoologists observing wildlife. It was up to me to end this disaster.

I cast a calming spell, unsure if it would work on someone who was undead. Carl did, in fact, slow down. Next, I expanded the spell to relax his muscles. The effect mimics the feeling you get in dreams like you're trying to walk through quicksand.

With a half-hearted groan of exhaustion, Carl sat on the floor amid the broken glass and pottery shards.

"Carl has never seen one of those creatures before," Madame Tibodet explained sheepishly.

And if you think this event was a nightmare, you should have seen Luisa's reaction when she arrived and saw the damage. Her carrying on made Carl look like the reasonable one.

Right in the middle of Luisa's tantrum was when Elizabeth Chubb arrived for the appointment I had completely forgotten about.

"Excuse me, is Missy Mindle here?" the overly thin blonde asked me, the proprietor who wasn't ranting. Carl had been sent home, and my handlers from the Society had wisely snuck out when no one was looking.

"That's me," I replied. "Oh my, are you Elizabeth? I'm so sorry. I lost track of the time."

"This is quite an unusual store."

"Yes, we cater to many spiritual beliefs."

"Spiritual? Okay. The reporter, Mr. Rosen, thought it would be better if I spoke to you, since you're a woman. But I thought you were his reporting partner. I didn't expect all"—she gestured at our wares—"this."

"Yes, we work together on many stories. I don't have a desk at the newsroom. I'm a freelance reporter. A stringer is what they call me. This, here, is my other job. It's hard to make a living in journalism these days."

"Okay, I understand now."

"Thank you so much for coming in here to speak with me. First, my condolences for your loss."

"I wish I could feel sorrow about Charles, but I can't," she said icily. "I'm fortunate he didn't do the same thing to me that happened to him."

"I understand."

"I'm afraid you don't. Two arrests and three restraining orders didn't stop him, even after he moved out. We have two children, and I was so frightened for their safety."

"Did he hurt them?"

"Thankfully, no. Not literally. I'd rather not talk about this."

"I'm sure the police have already questioned you," I said.

"Of course. I'm naturally their leading suspect, even though the kids and I were visiting my mother that night."

"Did you kill him?" I blurted out before I could stop myself.

She snorted. "I wasn't expecting such rudeness from you."

The problem with this interview was that I knew Matt wanted me to use my truth spell on Elizabeth. But I didn't like to use that spell unless I believed someone was guilty or lying to me. I didn't think Elizabeth was either.

"Do any suspects come to mind?" I asked. "You know, like loan sharks or the husband of someone he was seeing? Or a friend of yours who took matters into his own hands?"

She shook her head and seemed to close off to me. I guess I wasn't a good freelance reporter.

"There were no signs of forced entry at his condo," I said.

"Maybe someone ambushed him as he was coming home."

She glanced at her watch, as if she were about to leave. I changed my mind about using the truth spell and quickly conjured it.

"Can you believe how much damage we had here today?" I asked to distract her.

She looked around at the mess that still hadn't been

cleaned up. At that exact moment, I sprinkled the powder that went with the spell on her feet.

A change swept over her face, and she became like the drunk person sitting next to you at the bar who has so much they can't wait to tell you.

"I will ask you again," I said. "Did you kill Charles?"

"No. He's put me in the emergency room, and, yes, I fantasized about putting him in his grave. But what I truly wanted was to put the violent pig in prison. That's all."

"Do you know who killed him?"

"No, I don't."

"Was Charles having an affair?"

"I don't know, but I wouldn't be surprised if he was."

"Did he gamble? Do drugs? Or have large debts?"

"Not while we lived together."

"Do you have any suggestions of whom I should investigate?"

"Sorry. I wish I did, because I truly want you to find his killer. I want to give them an award."

And I wanted to keep Matt out of jail.

CHAPTER 8
SMOOTHIE OPERATOR

I was confident in the efficacy of my truth-telling spell, but sometimes the words you used when questioning suspects affected the results. They might answer you truthfully, but only in the narrowest, most literal sense.

So, lacking any leads, I followed Elizabeth after she left the botanica. Perhaps, she knew something, and I hadn't asked the right questions to reveal it.

She drove south from Jellyfish Beach, even though Matt had told me she lived in town. Obviously, she had an errand to do. Was I wasting my time following her to a dentist appointment?

Soon, we entered Port Inferno, and when she turned onto the road leading to the park and boat ramp, I knew something was up. Why would she go to a park so far out of her way?

Matt, I reminded myself, often paddleboarded here. I guess it was a good spot for the sport. Was it why she drove here?

This time of day, in the middle of the week, few people were at the park. I had to keep my car far behind hers so she wouldn't spot me. She pulled into a parking spot far from the boat ramp, near a small convenience store. I parked behind a tree, where I was half hidden but could still observe her.

She walked into the store, which sold overpriced drinks, snacks, and bait. It also rented out kayaks and paddleboards.

I knew little about her, other than she was a marketing executive and should be at work now instead of at a place that today had mostly vacationers and retirees.

Larry, the toothless old crabber I'd seen before, rode a bicycle past my car and stopped by the pier next to the boat ramp. His bike had two fishing rods in rod holders made from PVC pipes attached to the rear of his bike. He walked into the store carrying a bait bucket.

Finally, Elizabeth emerged from the building, sipping a smoothie in a plastic cup. Immediately after she came out, a man exited the store. My breath stopped when I recognized him.

It was Burt Umber, crabber, migrant smuggler, and enemy of Jerome Puttle, the first murder victim.

He must have bonded out of jail. Had he spoken to Elizabeth inside the store?

Was it just a coincidence that two people with ties to two different murders were in the same place at the same time?

I quickly searched the internet for Charles Chubb, her husband, and *The Jellyfish Beach Journal's* stories about his murder. Social media, too. There was no mention of him being a boater, fisherman, crabber, or anything that would put him within Burt Umber's orbit.

I did the same for Elizabeth Chubb. I found a lot of stuff related to her marketing career and some social media posts about paddleboarding. Was the water sport the only reason she was familiar with this park?

She returned to her car, and Umber got into a red pickup truck nearby. The toothless guy exited the store with his bait bucket, grabbed his two fishing rods from his bicycle, and walked to the end of the pier.

I briefly considered confronting Elizabeth and giving her another truth spell, but I believed she would react badly once she realized I had followed her here.

Instead, I continued to tail her as she returned to Jellyfish Beach. She drove to a modern office building near the interstate highway and went inside. After an hour, she hadn't come out, so I grew restless and drove home.

If she knew Burt Umber, that could tie her husband's murder with Puttle's. Assuming, of course, that Umber's alibi for Puttle's murder was a lie.

I needed to connect the dots here somehow. The dots were just too darn far apart.

"Burt Umber and Elizabeth Chubb were meeting?" Matt asked when I told him about my little surveillance trip.

"I didn't say they were meeting. I said they were in the same place at the same time. Could be a complete coincidence."

"But why was she even at the park in Port Inferno?"

"Her social media has photos of her paddleboarding. Maybe she goes to the park like you because it's a good location for that. And today, she had a craving for one of their smoothies."

"I didn't even know they made smoothies. I don't think I'd want a smoothie from a place that sells live shrimp for bait."

"It seemed to taste good enough for her."

"She must have been meeting with him," Matt insisted. "Okay, I know I sound desperate to find a connection between the Puttle and Chubb murders, because right now, I'm the only connection."

"Why do they have to be connected?"

"Because murders are still rare enough in this town that two in such a short timeframe ought to be connected."

"As far as I'm concerned, the only thing they have in common is the fact that a gun or knife wasn't used," I said. "The articles you wrote about them are irrelevant."

"In Detective Shortle's eyes, what I wrote 'showed moral outrage'—Shortle's words. I'm a crusading journalist whose anger pushed me over the edge and made me take the law into my own hands."

"Really? How often does that happen in the real world?"

"I haven't heard about journalists becoming violent vigilantes. At least, not in this country, or in this century."

"Shortle's guilty of the same mistake we were talking about —wanting there to be a connection between the two murders when there isn't one. In fact," I said, "you could just as easily blame a cop, like Shortle."

"What?"

"Yeah, she's the one who was morally outraged. She couldn't find a way to take down Puttle legally for endangering his kid, or Chubb for beating his wife. So, she took care of them extrajudicially."

"Shortle stuffed a guy in a crab trap and bashed in a head with a statuette?"

"Yeah. Everyone would assume a cop would use her weapon, not her bare hands. She's not a weakling, you know."

Matt sighed. "I think we're drifting into nutty conspiracy-theory land."

"Agreed. Jellyfish Beach simply had two unrelated murders in the same week."

Matt was silent.

"Are you good with that?" I asked.

"There *has* to be a connection between Burt Umber and Elizabeth Chubb."

"Here we go again."

"She's having an affair with him, and after he killed his nemesis, Puttle, she told him, while he was at it, to get rid of her husband, too. You need to cast your truth spell on her again and ask her about Umber."

"I don't feel comfortable doing that for such a crazy hypothesis."

"You'd rather I get arrested?"

"Don't be overly dramatic."

"Sorry, I'm a crusading journalist." He paused. "Please help me, Missy."

"Okay, okay. I'll talk to her again. Let's meet for breakfast tomorrow so we can discuss the angle I'll use."

"Sure. Let's make it early. Seven o'clock. I'm going surf-fishing before dawn, so I'll be near the cafe."

I agreed. I hoped to talk more sense into him and get him out of his paranoid mindset.

Little did I know that his paranoia was justified.

I SHOWED up at The Pasture in between lunch and dinner, when I knew Trevor would be there, but few staff. The centaur, actually a hybrid creature created through voodoo magic, had become a bit of a local celebrity. His "farm to fork" vegetarian restaurant was a big hit. Somehow, he had kept secret from the public that he was a horse from the waist down.

The manager knew of Trevor's secret, and that we were friends, so she allowed me to look for him in the kitchen.

"Missy! Good to see you," Trevor said as he chopped carrots. Standing behind the prep counter, his horse half was hidden, and he looked like a normal, handsome human. He used strategic placements like this to hide his true nature from most people, except for his closest staff.

"Good to see you, too, Trevor. I'm afraid that I'm here to ask a favor."

"A catering job?"

"No. I need you to do a little show-and-tell session with an evil black-magic sorceress."

"Say what?"

I explained my mission to infiltrate the coven and Ruth's demands that I prove my loyalty.

"But why me?" he asked.

I told him about Hercules's Twelve Labors, some of which included capturing mythical creatures, and that Trevor would be one of my versions of the labors.

"What does she want from me?"

"Nothing, I think. The whole thing is performative—I must take you to her to demonstrate the lengths I will go to please her. I just need you to say hello, that's all."

"Sounds suspicious to me. I'm not a carnival freak, you know."

"Of course. I'm sorry. This is such an awkward request."

"It is," he said, gripping his knife a little too firmly. "But I feel obligated to help you after all you've done for me."

His grip on the knife relaxed, and he set it down on the cutting board.

"Okay. After we close tonight, I'll have my driver take me. But you'll be there, too, right?"

"Yes, of course."

"I'm not going inside her place. I'm staying in the van."

"Thank you so much!"

I gave him her address and told him I'd bring Ruth downstairs to see him in the van.

"I'll make this as painless as possible."

Famous last words.

TREVOR HAD a driver in his employ, which shows you how successful he was. He didn't have a choice, though, other than customizing a van that he could drive himself, standing up, with his hoof operating the brake and accelerator. But this van was first-class, with a comfortable upholstered stall in the back for Trevor, complete with a video screen and minibar.

It had taken me quite a lot of sweet talking to persuade Ruth to come down to the street to meet Trevor. She had insisted that I take him to her apartment and present him like a tribute to Her Holiness. But I convinced her that a half-horse creature simply wouldn't fit in the building's small elevator or maneuver easily up the stairs.

"Well, well, isn't he precious?" she cooed after Trevor's driver slid open the side door of the van, revealing its passenger. She looked him up and down. "Shouldn't you wear a jockstrap, at least?"

"My lower half is as it should be," he said, though he wore a T-shirt and sport coat on his upper half. "*Au naturel.*"

"Can I pet you?"

"I'd rather you not."

"Missy said that you were made with voodoo. Is that right?"

Trevor winced. "With magic from a voodoo sorcerer, but it wasn't voodoo per se. It was a magical form of gene editing."

"How interesting. But however you were made, you suit my needs just fine."

"What needs?" I asked. "He's here just to meet you, that's all."

"Centaur blood is one of the most prized ingredients in black magic," Ruth said in a husky voice. "I have longed for some of it my entire career."

"Okay, Wilbur," Trevor said to his driver. "We're out of here."

The driver slid the van's door closed and got into the driver's seat, starting the engine.

"He's leaving already?" Ruth said in a childish voice. "I can't have that."

The van's engine died.

I sensed Ruth's magic in the air and frantically cast a protection spell for Trevor.

80

The van's side door slid open on its own. Ruth had a maniacal grin as she pointed to Trevor cowering in the back.

"Don't, Saint Ruthless," I said. "I gave my word that he would be safe. Leave him alone, or I won't join your coven."

"Your choice was to join or die. If you choose to die, that's your problem."

Simultaneously, while maintaining the protection spell, I cast a sleep spell on Ruth.

It obviously didn't work. While the driver impotently tried to start the van, Ruth marched toward Trevor with a knife that had mysteriously appeared in her hand.

"No!" I shouted as I dove at her, grabbing the wrist of her knife hand.

I wasn't much for attack spells, so brute force was all I had.

With inhuman strength, she swept her arm to the side, flinging me onto the sidewalk.

It looked like Trevor had been about to flee on hoof from the van, but Ruth must have paralyzed him. He stood there, frozen with fear except for his chest rising and falling with his hyperventilation.

Ruth leaned into the van and thrust her knife at Trevor's haunch. It bounced off the protection bubble from my spell.

"Nice try, dearie," she said to me. "I'll destroy your spell in just a minute."

There wasn't much time, but I had to cast one of the spells Angela had taught me that were based on the elements my magic was attuned to.

"Help me, Wilbur!" Trevor said through immobile jaws.

The driver rushed out of the front seat with a handgun. But not quickly enough. He froze, paralyzed.

I concentrated on my spell, knowing all the energy I needed would compromise my protection spell. But I had no choice.

"Oh goody," Ruth cackled. "Your silly protection bubble is fading already."

My ears buzzed as my entire body vibrated from all my gathered energy. And then, I cast the spell.

A precisely targeted micro-gust of wind swept past the van and hit Ruth, blowing her off her feet and carrying her to the front door of her building, where she crashed face-first with tremendous force.

Of the five magical elements, wind and earth were my affinities. This wind spell was just one example of what I could do with my power.

Ruth's collision with the front door broke her concentration and released the spells she'd been using. Wilbur and Trevor were freed from paralysis.

"Quick, get out of here!" I shouted to the driver.

He jumped back into the van, and it started immediately.

"I'm so sorry, Trevor," I said, as the side door slid shut and the van sped away.

No more discounted meals at The Pasture for me.

Ruth groaned on the front stoop of her building. I had worried, after she landed, that I had broken her neck or something else serious. Was it a sin to hurt someone who was evil?

Sin or not was irrelevant. I was a nurse by trade, and I had sworn to do no harm.

So, I walked over to my adversary to check on her. She had a large bruise on her forehead, but not readily apparent broken bones. I'd need to examine her more thoroughly to assess her injuries.

She appeared to be coming out of a daze.

"Very impressive, dearie," she mumbled. "Should I applaud you, or kill you?"

"You asked me to bring you a centaur to test my loyalty. I did what you requested. But I also promised Trevor that no harm would come to him. You hid from me your plan to hurt him."

"Just a blood donation. That's all I asked for."

"I honored my promise to him," I said sternly. "Same with my promise to you. As you can see, I'm loyal to those who trust me."

Ruth cackled and spat out a tooth.

"Oh, sorry about that," I said.

"I can fix it with my magic. As you'll learn, there's so much power in black magic."

"As I'll learn?"

"Yes. You've proven your loyalty by honoring your word. We shall proceed with your training. As soon as you accomplish another task."

"Another one? Why?"

"Hercules had to do twelve. Surely, you can do more than one."

"What is it?"

"I'll let you know as soon as I figure it out."

I examined her as best I could, there on the top of the steps, without medical equipment. She appeared to only have some contusions. Perhaps with all her energy going into her spells, her body had been limp, and thus less prone to damage when she hit the door.

Or the old bag was simply indestructible.

"You should stop by the ER and have them check you out," I said.

"Nah, I'm fine. I need to cast a spell to fix this tooth before it dies."

"Again, I'm sorry about the tooth."

"Hate means never having to say you're sorry."

I didn't feel any hate, really. At least, not yet.

That would change very soon.

CHAPTER 9
FATAL FISHING

Good thing I grabbed an outside table at the cafe the following morning. Matt was a little—how do I put this—stinky. He reeked of fish.

"I take it you were successful this morning," I said.

"Yeah. I caught some whiting and croakers. I kept a few. They're in my cooler, in case you want to join me for a fish fry tonight."

"Sounds good. Is that blood on your shirt?"

"Fish blood. And probably some of mine, too." He held up his hand to show me a nasty laceration between his thumb and forefinger, running from his palm to the back of his hand. "My braided fishing line did this."

"Oh my. You're a mess." I handed him an adhesive bandage and a bottle of hand sanitizer from my purse. I'm a nurse, after all.

"I used the shower at the beach to get most of the fish

blood and slime off me, but I'll have to put this shirt through the washer with bleach to remove the stains."

It was just after dawn, and the cafe was the only beachside business open at this hour. No one was swimming in the ocean, but there were plenty of walkers and joggers on the sidewalk beside the dunes.

The server dropped off Matt's coffee and my tea. The coffee's aroma helped mask Matt's fishy smell.

I asked Matt why he was brooding.

"Surf fishing before dawn is a great way to remove stress and enjoy the beach when no one is around. Catching fresh fish is a bonus. But today, I came across a couple of shark fishermen. I *hate* them. Shark fishing from the beach is illegal now in Jellyfish Beach, but people do it anyway because there's no enforcement. It almost always kills the sharks from the stress of being landed on the beach. Pointless deaths, because most of these fishermen don't eat them."

"That's sad," I said.

"There were two guys. One of them went home, but the other one kept fishing. He looked familiar, and I remembered interviewing him a while back for a story about surf fishing for sharks. I asked him why he still did it. He said he did it for the adrenaline rush and for the photos to post on social media. Disgusting."

"Yeah. You've often complained about shark fishing from the beach."

"I sure have. I wrote several pieces about it, all told. It's not bragging to say that my exposure is part of the reason the city passed the ordinance banning the practice. It's not just the cruelty, it's also the danger of attracting sharks to a swimming beach. You know, they usually throw chum in the water to bring the sharks closer to shore."

I shuddered. "Yeah, I don't want to think of sharks where I go swimming."

"Exactly." He continued brooding.

"You did a good thing bringing attention to this matter," I said, hoping to cheer him up.

But just as our food arrived, sirens pierced the morning quiet.

An ambulance and fire truck sped past the cafe, followed by a police car. They stopped at a dune crossover not far from the cafe.

"I hope a swimmer didn't drown," I said. "Or wasn't attacked by a shark."

"They stopped near the spot where I was fishing. I didn't see anyone around when I left. Except for the remaining shark fisherman."

It was hard to enjoy my meal with the flashing lights visible just up the street. Matt kept glancing at his phone, checking for news updates. I knew he was dying to see what was happening on the beach but didn't want to be rude to me.

"You can go check it out," I said. "I'll take care of the bill."

Like a dog released from his leash, Matt walked, then sprinted toward the action. I had a few more bites of my French toast, then signaled the server for the check. After I paid, I headed toward the beach. I admit the curiosity was getting to me. Even though it was the kind that made you stare at a car wreck.

I couldn't help but walk quickly as the curiosity over-whelmed me. By the time I reached the area where the emergency vehicles had pulled over, the medical examiner's SUV had arrived as well, along with Shortle's car.

Uh-oh. This didn't appear to be a drowning or shark attack. It was more likely a crime caused by a human.

Two techs, a man and a woman, struggled to wheel a gurney over the sandy path that led through the dunes. On it was a body bag zippered shut with a rotund figure inside.

Uh-oh.

When I reached the beach, the crime-scene techs crouched on the sand near abandoned fishing gear. Matt hovered over them, asking questions. Beachgoers were showing up as the morning advanced, and two uniformed officers kept them away from the crime scene.

Bird was among the officers. She nodded at me without the slightest hint of a smile.

Detective Shortle interviewed an older couple who appeared distraught, as if they had discovered the body. She kept glancing at Matt, who was keeping a wary eye on her.

When Shortle dismissed the couple, she ambled over to Matt, who was pestering the crime-scene techs. I followed her so I could eavesdrop on the conversation.

"Why am I not surprised to see you again, Rosen?" Shortle asked.

"Yeah, funny, isn't it? Let me be upfront about my involvement. I was fishing here early this morning and saw the victim and his friend catching and killing a shark. After the friend left, the victim moved his location closer to me. So, I had a few words with him."

"Just words?"

"Of course. I'm opposed to surf fishing for sharks. In fact, my investigative series in the *Journal* contributed to the ban the city passed last year."

"You're a crusader, all right." Her voice was dripping with sarcasm.

"Um, yeah. And I think I should point out that I interviewed the victim back when I was reporting on that series. I wanted to point that out before you read the articles. If you read them."

"I certainly will now."

"And the victim was still fishing here when I left the beach," Matt added.

"Where did you go then?"

"I met Ms. Mindle at the Undertow Cafe. That's where we were when the emergency vehicles showed up, and I came back here to see what had happened."

"Of course, you had nothing to do with what happened. Is that what you're going to tell me?"

"Yeah. The victim was standing here fishing."

"Why do you have blood on your shirt?"

"It's fish blood. And maybe a little of mine from my hand."

"How did you get that cut?"

"A big bluefish hit my lure while I was trying to untangle my line, and it got wrapped around my hand. This nylon braided line is really low diameter and super strong. It'll cut right into you."

"I'm going to have to take your shirt so the lab can test the blood," Shortle said with her hand out.

"Right now?"

"Yes."

Matt removed his shirt with the body language of someone being strip searched, even though he normally had no issue with doing water sports in nothing more than a bathing suit. He wasn't bad-looking shirtless, I should add. He was hardly a bodybuilder, but his lean body had well-defined pecs and abs. Just saying.

He handed over the wrinkled white shirt with all the little pockets that fishermen seem to like.

Shortle wrinkled her nose. "Between you and the fish you caught, this shirt is pungent."

"Sure, Detective, humiliate me some more."

"Oh, you haven't seen anything yet. Before I let you go, did anyone witness you fishing on the beach? Aside from the victim?"

"His buddy probably saw me. They were further north from me at the time, and I can't swear he'd recognize me. It was still pretty dark when he left."

I looked around for security cameras or webcams. I couldn't see any. The main public beach was down by the cafe, and there were webcams mounted on a nearby condo building. You could find the footage on the city's website and on surfing sites.

Here at the crime scene, there were no buildings or homes with unobstructed views of this spot. Unless there were hidden cameras somewhere, there would be no video of the murder to back up Matt's claims that he wasn't here. Which was unfortunate.

Unless Matt was guilty. In that case, he was very lucky there were no cameras.

Wait, how could I even think such a thought? Of course, Matt wasn't guilty.

"I need you to come chat with us again at the station,"

Shortle said to Matt. "I'll give you time to call your lawyer and run home to get a fresh shirt."

"How generous of you," I said.

Both Shortle and Matt glared at me. My attitude was not helping one bit. With that, Shortle marched away to speak with Officer Bird.

"I can't afford to antagonize Shortle," Matt said as we trudged back to the road and the parking lot behind the cafe.

"I know. I'm sorry. By the way, did you find out how the fisherman died?"

"Strangled with his own fishing line. Garroted would better describe it." He held up his wounded hand. "He must have been using braided line, too."

"Thanks for the graphic description."

"I guess it's not a good look for me that I cut my hand with fishing line, given that the victim died that way."

"No. Thankfully, you have an attorney."

"You're not very good at making me feel better."

"What's the victim's name?"

"Why?"

"Someone needs to find out who else would want to kill him."

"Who *else*? You mean, who else besides a 'crusading journalist' who can't control his temper?"

"Basically, yes."

"Billy Lee Jacobs. I couldn't remember off the top of my head, but a cop at the scene was kind enough to tell me. That was before I looked like the murderer."

"The best thing you can do is to not act like a murderer.

Don't talk to Shortle without Paul. Meanwhile, I'll investigate Jacobs. How do we find out who his friend was?"

"Look up the articles I wrote last year. He may have been mentioned in the one where I interviewed Jacobs. The guy I saw this morning looked familiar: heavy and tall with dark hair and a huge beard. I think there was a photo of both of them in the article."

I called Luisa to tell her I'd be late showing up at the botanica, and I followed Matt to his bungalow so I could keep asking questions before his police interview. He called Paul Leclerc, who said he'd adjust his schedule and meet us at the station in an hour.

"I should shower," Matt said.

"Who cares if Shortle thinks you smell?"

"It might be the last shower I get for a while."

"Oh, please, don't be fatalistic."

"I'm being realistic," he replied from his bedroom with its door opened a crack.

Soon, I heard the shower running. An idea popped into my head that embarrassed me. It involved taking off my clothes and slipping into the shower with Matt. After all, if he was truly afraid of losing his freedom . . .

No, it wasn't a Missy Mindle kind of thing to do. I was a nerd, obsessed with magic and medicine. I hadn't done a thing like that since my honeymoon so many years ago.

That didn't mean I couldn't imagine doing it. It didn't mean that by the time Matt emerged from his bedroom, wearing new clothes and smelling of soap and shampoo, I wouldn't want to kiss him.

Which I did. As soon as he emerged from his bedroom.

"Whoa," he said when I pulled my lips and tongue away, "what is this for? You, too, think I'm going to the clink?"

"No. Just wanted to show you how much I care about you in this difficult time."

"The feeling is likewise."

He pulled me in tight and kissed me, almost desperately.

"We have time for more," I said. "The drive to the police station is short."

"I don't think I can focus right now. Maybe, they'll allow us a conjugal visit while I'm in the state pen."

"Please stop talking that way," I said, peeling myself away from him. "You're innocent, you have a good lawyer, and you should have nothing to fear."

"'Should' is doing a lot of work there."

"You need to have faith your innocence will prevail. If Shortle senses fear in you, she'll be a shark smelling blood in the water."

"Apt metaphor."

"Come on," I said, taking his hand. "I'll drive you to the station."

"No, please don't come. I don't want you to go through that. I could be there for hours. Or days. I don't want to worry about you waiting for me in some uncomfortable plastic chair. Please, go to work, and I'll call you to let you know how it went."

Reluctantly, I agreed. I gave him a quick kiss and hug, wished him luck, then drove to the botanica.

Of course, I got little work done, with my mind whirling with theories. Fortunately, Luisa was there to serve customers while I sat at the front counter, clicking away on my laptop. A long-awaited shipment of newt tails and crow feathers arrived, but I left the box sitting on the counter while I searched *The Jellyfish Beach Journal's* archives.

I located and read Matt's articles from last year about the shark fishermen. They were well-reported and written, but as I read them, I couldn't help but wonder if the reporter sounded outraged enough to kill.

To be honest, he did.

CHAPTER 10
CRUSADING JOURNALIST

M att had written a half dozen articles about shark fishing. The first one appeared in the sports section of *The Journal*, and was largely positive, recounting the thrill of catching sharks, from makos to black fins, and releasing them alive and healthy. These adventures took place on boats that Matt was aboard.

The subsequent articles took a darker turn as Matt investigated those who caught sharks from jetties and piers, where the sharks could still be released alive, but it was riskier for the creatures.

Finally, when he explored shark fishing from the beach, the crusading journalist in him came to the fore as he pointed out that most of the sharks died from the stress of the long struggle as they were pulled to shore and dragged out of the water up onto the sand. Even if they were still alive, getting them back into the water, and helping them swim away, was usually unsuccessful.

I found the article that featured the victim, Billy Lee Jacobs. Matt had interviewed both him and his fishing partner, Todd Oddbelly. In a photo of the two men holding rods, silhouetted by a beautiful sunrise, the man standing beside Jacobs was tall, heavy, and bearded, with black hair. He matched the description of the man Matt saw with Jacobs on the fateful morning.

Since I was reading an online version of the article, beneath it were comments posted by readers. A few were sympathetic, but most lambasted the two fishermen for their cruelty and indifference to the health of the shark population. Others rang the alarm about the safety concerns for swimmers.

Had Shortle read these comments? Any of the individuals who left these posts could have been the murderer. Unfortunately, I had no way of figuring out the real names behind their online usernames, but perhaps the police could get into the website's registration records.

That is, if Shortle wanted to. This last shark story by Matt had strayed from his usual objectivity into barely concealed anger and contempt. Anyone reading this story would doubt Matt had shed any tears after one of these fishermen turned up dead.

Still, we have the right to free speech in this country. The police can't arrest you for something you write, as long as it's not a death threat.

Or can they?

My phone rang. It was Paul Leclerc. I answered it with my heart pounding.

"Hey, Missy, it's Paul. I'm sorry to inform you that Matt has been taken into custody."

"You mean arrested?"

"Yes."

"They're accusing him of murdering the fisherman?"

"Yes, along with the crabber and the wife abuser."

"Based on what evidence?" I was almost shouting. "They have no evidence! All they have is the coincidence that Matt wrote stories about them. And had an argument with Puttle. This is a small city, and Matt has worked at the newspaper for years. He's probably written about almost everybody."

"Shortle and the state attorney are grasping at straws regarding the first two deaths. But Shortle located Jacobs' fishing partner, and he claims Matt accosted them and threatened their lives that morning."

"Bull pucky!" I shouted, which was as close to swearing as I ever got. "Matt would never do that. Why did Oddbelly lie about him?"

"Oh, you discovered his name?"

"Yeah. Obviously too late to reach out to him and get the truth."

"I don't know why he would lie. Shortle probably encouraged him to. Based on Matt's account, if Oddbelly had seen Matt at all, it was from a distance. Maybe, the guy's an inveterate liar and elaborated on the information Shortle fed him."

"Still, there's no reason for him to make up a story about an innocent man. I'm going to track him down and speak to him."

"You mean use a little magic on him?"

"Exactly."

"Normally, I would advise you against tampering with a witness," Paul said. "But this guy is such a liar. If you do speak to him, be sure to erase his memory of meeting with you to avoid getting into trouble with the authorities."

"I sure will. Can I speak to Matt?"

"He's being booked right now. He said he'll call you when he has access to a phone."

I thanked Paul and felt tears rolling down my cheeks.

"What's wrong?" Luisa asked.

I gave her a condensed version of the story.

"*Dios mio!*" she exclaimed. "That's horrible! I'm so sorry. Will you use your magic to break him out of jail?"

"Of course not! I don't even believe I could. Well, actually, with the right combination of spells . . . No, I can't go there."

"Yes, that would be problematic for both of you."

"I'm going to have to trust that Paul Leclerc lives up to his reputation as a good defense attorney. But I'll also have to continue what I've been doing so much lately."

"Looking for monsters while neglecting your duties here?"

"Very funny. I'll try to find the actual murderer or murderers."

"You won't have Matt to help you investigate."

"I've done a lot more of that than you realize."

"I wish you the best of luck, and I'm here to help you in any way. Would you like me to pray to the Orishas for you?"

"The more help, the better."

AS THE PROSECUTION team moved toward trial, they would be required to give Paul information about their star witness, Todd Oddbelly. But I couldn't wait that long. To locate him, I would have to rely on my own resources. I started with the internet, and it didn't let me down. Searching public records yielded Oddbelly's address in a court document.

It turned out he owned a company called Todd's Towing. It had an address in Port Inferno that sounded residential. I headed there as soon as I got off work.

What was it about Port Inferno that created so many connections with the recent murders? Besides Oddbelly, Puttle and Umber were from the town, and even Elizabeth Chubb had some inexplicable reason for driving to the park at the same time Umber was there. I would have to see if Jacobs had lived there, too.

Oddbelly's address was in a working-class neighborhood of single-family homes like Puttle's. A tow truck was parked in the driveway, but no one answered the doorbell. I sat in my car, parked along the curb, hoping he returned home soon.

After about an hour, a brown SUV pulled into the driveway beside the tow truck. A large man that I recognized as Oddbelly from the photograph climbed out and helped three young children out of the back seat.

"Let's get dinner going before Mommy comes home," he said to his kids as he led them through the front door.

It was difficult to resolve the family man I just saw with the man who had lied for no reason and got Matt arrested. But the fact that he was a father didn't stop me from wanting to take him down, if necessary.

I had a feeling it would be best to use my magic on him before his wife got home, to more effectively make him confess he'd lied. He was also probably distracted by his kids right now, which would make him more vulnerable.

It was time to act. I got out of my car and hurried to the

front door, not exactly sure what my sales pitch would be to give me enough time to enchant him and sprinkle the magic dust.

Only two seconds after I rang the doorbell, the door opened. The tall, bearded man looked at me with surprise.

"Oh. I thought you were my neighbor," he said, moving to close the door.

"Wait! I have a quick question for you—"

The door shut in my face. I rang the bell again. The door opened a crack.

"What do you want? I'm not donating to your kid's soccer team."

"I'm a reporter with *The Jellyfish Beach Journal*," I lied. "I just want—"

"No comment." He slammed the door closed.

This was a problem. I knew I could get inside and incapacitate him via various spells, but I'd be breaking the law. Besides, my truth spell worked better when the subject wasn't under duress. I was in a pickle.

What was I supposed to do? I couldn't call him, because my truth spell wouldn't work over the phone.

A compact car arrived and parked in the driveway behind the SUV. A wiry, exhausted-looking woman got out. His wife, no doubt. I got the feeling she was the main breadwinner for the family, while her husband spent his time fishing and waiting for towing requests to come in.

I intercepted her on her way to the front door.

"Excuse me, ma'am," I said.

She stopped and looked at me like she was about to deck me.

"I'm not donating to your kid's soccer team," she said with a snarl.

"My name is Missy Mindle. I'm a reporter with *The Jellyfish Beach Journal*. Your husband is accused of giving false statements to the police, and I wanted to give him a chance to clear his name. But he won't open the door for me."

The woman looked me up and down suspiciously. "He don't wanna talk. His best friend was murdered. Give the man a break."

"I'm giving him the opportunity to tell his side of the story before the police charge him with the murder."

I was just making up stuff as I went along—anything for a minute or two face to face with her husband.

"Todd!" she yelled after opening the door. "There's a reporter here who says you got to talk to her before the police charge you with murder."

"Say what?"

He came to the door.

If I could only get the wife out of the way, I could sprinkle the magic powder on his feet and ask him what had really happened on the beach.

"I didn't kill nobody," he said.

"I know, but the police think you lied to them," I said, lying through my teeth.

"It's none of your business. Get off our lawn before I shoot you."

With a squeal, a toddler-aged little boy ran out the door wearing only diapers. The wife raced after him.

I moved toward Oddbelly as he stood in the doorway, gaping at the chase scene.

But then, another child, a boy about six years old, jumped outside with a water blaster and soaked me with water.

"Good boy, Jason! Blast that bad woman!"

"You're not setting a good example," I said, a second stream of water hitting my face.

The kid was an excellent marksman. I retreated.

Now, a third kid and a dog were romping in the front yard while the mother captured the diaper-clad toddler.

After a third jet of water hit my head, I realized it was time to retreat. I had failed in my mission.

I would have to report my failure to Matt when we spoke. Later that evening, my phone rang, and a recorded voice said, "This is a collect call from an inmate at the Crab County Jail. Do you accept the charges?"

"Yes," I replied.

"Missy, you've got to get me out of here," Matt said in an overly calm voice.

"I'm trying," I said. "I want to get the second fisherman to admit he lied about you attacking them. I haven't been successful."

"They have no evidence against me, except his testimony. Everything else is just circumstantial—just coincidences."

"Yes, I know. What about the blood on your shirt?"

"What do you mean? I told you it was fish blood and my blood. You think I'm lying?"

"No. I mean, did the report come back yet to prove that?"

"I don't know. When are you going to talk to the other fisherman? What's his name again?"

"Todd Oddbelly. I tried and failed tonight. But don't worry,

I'll get to him. I promise. Now, tell me, how are you holding up?"

"It's a nightmare in here. And there's a man waiting to use the phone who said he's going to turn me into a human pretzel if I don't end my call. I'll call you back soon."

"Okay, Matt. I lo—"

He hung up before I could use the L word.

Perhaps that was for the best. A collect call from the county jail was not the best forum for taking our relationship to the next level.

After an unenjoyable meal of leftovers, I permitted myself a long soak in the tub with a glass of wine. Once I was relaxed, I thought of an easy way to talk to Todd Oddbelly.

It was so obvious. Why hadn't I thought of it sooner?

CHAPTER 11

GO WITH THE TOW

"Someone parked their piece-of-junk car in my driveway and left it there. I don't know who it was. I need this wreck towed," I said when I called Todd's Towing the next morning.

"All right. What's your name and address?"

"Um, Susan Sorceress." I cringed at such a lame attempt at a fake name. "Sixteen Ibis Drive."

"If I need to, can I reach you at this number?"

"Yep."

"I'm handling a job right now. When I'm done, later this morning, I'll be there."

Before he hung up, the sounds of wind and crashing surf were in the background. It sounded like the "job" he was handling was fishing.

While I waited for him to arrive, I sipped hot tea at my kitchen table and thought about the three recent murders that appeared unrelated, but somehow were tied to Matt.

"You can bounce ideas off me," said Tony, my iguana witch's familiar. He had suddenly appeared on the island counter.

"You were reading my thoughts?" I asked.

"Yup. That's what a good witch's familiar does," he replied in his New York accent. "Telepathy helps me serve you better. Now, why are they accusing Pencil Neck of the crimes?"

"His name is Matt. And I guess Detective Shortle has issues with him and his aggressive reporting."

"Issues?"

"The victims were not good people, and Matt just happened to have written articles about them in the past that were highly critical. The first victim, Puttle, had been in trouble with the law before, but the most recent thing he did was discharge his shotgun in his young child's room, just a few feet from his bed."

"This is the dude who killed the crested mouth sprite?"

"Right."

"Matt was allegedly upset about that?"

"He was upset about the recklessness of endangering the kid. We all were."

"Gotcha."

"Then, the guy allegedly fired shots into Matt's bungalow."

"Ah. Which would understandably make Matt upset."

"Yes. Understandably. The next victim was abusing his wife. Matt had covered the man's various arrests for doing the same thing."

"Okay."

"The most recent victim was killed on the beach while illegally shark fishing. Matt had previously written about him in an article criticizing the practice. The victim's fishing buddy claimed that Matt had threatened them. This is the case that puts Matt in the most jeopardy because of the witness testimony. They could prosecute him for this, even if they don't charge him in the other cases."

"So, the police believe Matt is a psycho vigilante who goes around killing people he doesn't approve of?"

"Basically."

"I don't buy it."

"Neither do I. The theory is absurd."

"Right. Matt is too much of a wimp to do something like that."

"Watch it," I said. "Poor Matt is in jail right now. The theory is absurd because it tries to link unrelated murders with an illogical motive."

"Psychopaths aren't logical," Tony said. "They kill people for the most unlikely of reasons. They kill people who remind them of someone. Or are a certain age. Or have a certain hair color. The victims aren't even humans to the killers. They're just objects."

"Matt is not a psychopath."

"He's been good at hiding it all these years."

"Whose side are you on, you silly lizard?"

"Look, you've said the detective is inexperienced, right?"

"Yeah. Though she's had more than her share of murders to deal with since she moved here."

"I'm sure she took classes in serial killers and psychopaths. She's probably eager to put that knowledge to work. She'd rather assume these murders are by a serial killer instead of more mundane actors."

"You might be right, but I would have thought Detective Glasbag would have advised her against that. He's not very bright, but he's much more experienced."

"Does he like Matt?"

"No. He thinks Matt is a pest."

"What a surprise! Knock me over with a feather."

"No one likes sarcastic reptiles."

"Does our brilliant police force have any other suspects?"

"If they do, they haven't said. The most obvious suspects have alibis."

"The alibis could be false. You need to look into that."

"Yeah." I rubbed my face, feeling stressed already. "I'm not used to investigating crimes without Matt. Don't forget, I also have a full-time job at the botanica and my home-health clients. Oh, and I run a weekly creative-writing class for vampires, which is tonight. How can I possibly give Matt the help he deserves?"

"You're a powerful witch, with a brilliant familiar. You've got this, girl."

The low rumbling of a diesel engine came from the front of the house. Todd's Towing was here.

I put on a baseball cap and dark shades, hoping he wouldn't recognize me from the chaos of last night. When I walked outside, he showed no signs of doing so.

"I don't blame you for wanting to get this wreck off your property," he said.

Of course, he was talking about my car, but I had to pretend otherwise. And later, I would have to pay a painful fee to get it back from the impoundment lot. Such were the sacrifices I was making for Matt.

I pulled out my phone and shot a video of the operation.

"I hope you don't mind that I'm recording this," I said. "I want to protect myself if the owner threatens to sue."

"The owners threaten lawsuits all the time," Oddbelly said. "They never win."

The truck hummed while its flatbed tilted backward toward my driveway. I stood as close to my car as I could without getting in the way. And I conjured the truth spell.

Once the flatbed had stopped moving, Oddbelly released the winch and pulled the cable toward my car. As he bent down to hook it up, I sprinkled the magic powder on his feet.

"Tell me the truth about what happened on the beach when Billy Lee Jacobs was murdered," I commanded.

"What are you talking about?" he asked.

But as he stood upright and looked at me, the telltale energy and the urge to talk were obvious in his face.

"Did a stranger with a beard really attack you and your fishing buddy."

"No, no. I made that up. Are you still filming me?"

"Yes, you'll be glad I did. You'll feel so much better when you unburden yourself and it's on record."

"Yeah, I've got to get this off my chest. There was a guy fishing just down the beach from us, but he didn't come over either time I was there."

"What do you mean by 'either time'?"

"I had to go home, but when I was halfway there, I realized I had left one of my rods at the beach. It's brand new. Cost me over three hundred bucks, including the reel. So, I went back to get it. But Billy Lee was using it and wouldn't let me have it."

"What did you do?"

"I snapped, I guess. Billy Lee and I were getting into a lot of arguments lately. He treated me like dirt. Thought he was better than me and always let me know it. When he started calling me names, I just lost it. Being as drunk as I was sort of erased my inhibitions. I strangled him with the fishing line: thirty-pound braid. Expensive stuff."

"*You* killed Billy Lee?"

"Yeah. I guess I feel kinda bad about it now."

"You *guess?*"

"Yeah. He had it coming to him, but maybe killing him was too much."

"*Maybe?*"

"So, when the police questioned me, I made it sound like that other guy on the beach was a maniac who was threatening us. I figured they'd think he killed Billy Lee."

"They did. And you'll tell them the truth now, right?"

"Yeah. It's the right thing to do."

"Yes, it is."

Paul had told me to use a forgetfulness spell so I wouldn't get in trouble for tampering with a witness. And I should have done so to make him forget to tow my car. But I didn't want Oddbelly to forget that he promised to confess to the police.

The winch pulled my poor car onto the flatbed. Oddbelly still had the animated look on his face that said the spell hadn't worn off yet. So, I asked what I've always wanted to ask one of these guys.

"Do you ever tow cars that aren't illegally parked, just for your share of the impoundment fees?"

"Yep. All the time."

"The police will contact you soon about Billy Lee," I said. "You *will* tell the truth."

"Yep. I will."

THE REST of my morning was spent taking a ride share to the impoundment lot, paying the exorbitant fee to get my car out, and driving myself back home. All this trouble just to get an opportunity to use my truth spell on Oddbelly. Thankfully, it had worked.

Since I had taken the morning off, I was supposed to work late and close the botanica. Then, I would go directly to Squid Tower for the creative-writing class. I was making a sandwich before heading to the shop when Ruth walked into my kitchen.

"Don't you ever ring the doorbell?" I asked.

"I shouldn't need your permission to enter. If you truly want to join my coven, what's yours is mine."

I was seriously questioning my mission to spy on her.

"Of course, come in whenever you like. Raid my fridge, take a shower, use my toothbrush. It's all yours."

"Sneering makes you unattractive, dearie."

"May I ask what brings you here? I have to go to work now."

"I've decided on the other task to prove your loyalty."

"Now is not a good time. I've got a lot on my plate."

"It is a daunting task, but if you complete it, it will bring a result you desire."

I sighed. "What is it?"

"I've heard through my informants that your friend and sweetheart is in jail. You will use your magic to free him."

Luisa had joked about that because it was, for real, a joke. Even if I could somehow get him out of the physical jail, we would have to live as fugitives. Besides, I didn't believe in using my magic for illegal purposes.

"That's impossible," I said.

"Not at all. You already know spells for unlocking doors, putting people to sleep, and immobilizing them. You could learn an invisibility spell and others that would come in handy."

I explained to her my taboo against using my magic for illegal acts.

"Do you believe your friend is innocent?"

"Of course."

"Then freeing him from unjust imprisonment can't be considered an illegal act."

"Tell that to the judge when I'm put on trial."

"Make sure you don't get caught."

"I'm hoping Matt won't need to escape. Thanks to my truth spell, I got the key witness against him to confess to the murder. If everything works out, Matt could walk."

"When the cops arrest someone, they don't like to admit they made a mistake. And maybe Matt is guilty of the other murders."

"No way."

"He's going to be behind bars for a long time, even if he's not convicted in the end. And if he *is* convicted . . ."

"Look, this is crazy talk. I'm not breaking Matt out of jail."

"Friends break their friends out of jail all the time. Well, at least in some countries."

"Not in this one. It never works out."

"You can argue with me all you want, but I've made up my mind. The task I have assigned you is to free your friend because it will test not only your loyalty to me, but also your magical powers. If you refuse to do it, you can't join my coven. And if you don't join, well, you already know the penalty for that."

"You're saying I must break Matt out of the county jail, or you'll kill me?"

"Yes. Saint Ruthless has spoken. May her will be done."

With that, she turned on her heel and strode out of my kitchen. Just as when she had arrived, she went through the front door without making a sound.

The pitter-patter of little clawed lizard feet approached from the door to the garage.

"Pretty exciting, huh?" Tony said. "A jailbreak! This will be your greatest magical achievement yet."

"I'm not breaking him out of jail. Period."

"I thought you were in love with Mr. Pencil Neck."

"Will you stop? If you've been reading my mind and eavesdropping on my conversations, you'd know that the key witness against Matt confessed to the murder."

"That's one of three murders, kiddo."

"There's hardly anything tying Matt to the other murders, and it's all circumstantial at best."

"That you're aware of. Who knows what the cops know?"

"Why is everyone being so pessimistic? You and my mother both."

"Because we want you to do the jailbreak. It's such an exciting challenge for our magical talents."

"You say 'our' talents. But I'll be the one who ends up getting arrested."

"Exactly. And I'll be fine. I'll find another witch who needs a familiar and doesn't want one that's a stupid cat."

"I'm tired of all this ridiculous talk. I need to get to the botanica. And remember, I'll be late coming home tonight."

"Guess I'll have to eat your neighbor's flowers for dinner."

What I didn't mention was I hoped to be at Squid Tower for a while after the class. I planned to seek advice from a certain ex-cop who had moved to Squid Tower after he was turned.

I needed all the help I could get.

CHAPTER 12
THERE ONCE WAS A MAN

W alt Whitman, world-famous undead poet, was reciting dirty limericks. This was the level of material I had to face weekly in the vampire creative-writing group.

Sol and Schwartz snickered at the scatological double-entendres. Gladys, who had just regaled us with another soft-core-porn erotic romance, smiled in appreciation. Everyone else, including me, was put off.

"Very witty, Walt," I said. "I never knew about this side of you."

"You thought I only wrote in free verse?"

"No, I thought you only wrote lofty, evocative, symbolic literature. You must admit, 'There Once Was a Man from Long Island' isn't on the same level as *Leaves of Grass*."

"As an artist, I reserve the right to evolve," he answered with a scowl.

"To devolve into an eight-year-old boy," Marjorie said.

"Remember," I said, "no personal attacks in this group."

"Let the guy write what he wants," Schwartz said. "This ain't a literary magazine. Now, it's my turn to read. My piece is a love story."

"You, Leonard Schwartz, wrote a love story?" Gladys asked.

"Yes. It's called 'For the Love of Schwartz.'"

And that's what it was. The short story had a thin plot about a young female human falling in love with an irascible old vampire, but it was, in essence, an essay about the author's awesomeness: how handsome, sexy, and charming he was to any woman willing to give him a chance.

After 175 years of existence, Schwartz had never been married. It was easy to see why.

In my years of serving the healthcare needs of vampires, I'd witnessed how the gift of eternal life affects their personalities. It's often not for the better.

Some vampires turn more feral after living more than a couple of centuries. Turned off by the constant changes in human culture and etiquette, they become alienated and more solitary. They devolve into creatures who only want to drink blood and sleep.

Other vampires, especially in a social community such as Squid Tower, become amplified versions of themselves. Each aspect of their personality becomes more extreme. For example, Schwartz, the narcissistic curmudgeon, became more, well, Schwartz.

I didn't know many freshly turned vampires, but unpleasant humans sometimes become more bearable once they're undead. A perfect example is former detective Fred Affird.

When he was alive, Affird was a jerk. One of the few humans who knew of the existence of vampires and other supernatural creatures, he used the power of his law-enforcement position to hunt, harass, and destroy these creatures.

He once extrajudicially executed a werewolf drug dealer at Seaweed Manor. And he was the bane of every vampire at Squid Tower.

Until they turned him.

You could say being undead mellowed Affird. First, it made him more tolerant of diversity, now that he was a minority. Also, staring into the face of eternity made him appreciate the subtle beauties of our world. In short, he was no longer such a jerk, though still far from the life of the party.

After the creative-writing session was over, I found Affird on the putting green next to the shuffleboard courts. He was hitting balls in the darkness, using his preternatural vampire vision.

"Hello, Missy. How are you?" he asked, recognizing me though I had approached him from behind.

"I'm okay, Detective. I've come seeking advice."

"That would be my pleasure."

Would it be an exaggeration to say the new-vampire Affird was a warm, avuncular guy? Maybe. But he was much more pleasant than the cruel, bitter man he used to be.

"I'm investigating some murders my friend, Matt Rosen, has been accused of," I explained.

"Rosen? The reporter? That annoying son of a . . ."

Okay, maybe Affird hadn't completely changed.

"Detective Shortle is trying to connect three unrelated murders on the theory they were committed by the same culprit. The only thing that connects them is the fact that Matt wrote critical articles about each of them."

"The victims were bad people?"

"You could say that."

"If so, there will be others who might have wanted to kill them," Affird said, making a perfect putt.

"That's what I'm thinking. And I might need a little help in finding the killer or killers."

"You need my detective skills?"

"That would be great if you're not too busy." I left unsaid that he was currently spending each night doing little more than killing time.

He stood straight and smiled. Light from a distant lamppost glinted off his fangs.

"Sometimes, I miss my old job," he said. "I was pretty good at it, you know, even though the crimes in this little burg didn't give me much of a challenge."

That's why he was so obsessed with harassing supernaturals.

"Your help would make such a difference," I said.

"I think Shortle is in over her head. But what do you expect when her only mentor is Marty Glasbag?" He snorted. "Trying to pin unrelated murders on a serial killer? This is Jellyfish Beach, not Miami. What are the odds that we have a serial killer here?"

"My thoughts exactly."

"When would you like to sit down and brief me on the cases?"

"Tomorrow night would be great. I've already made

tremendous progress in investigating the last murder. I got the actual murderer to confess, and I captured it on video."

"The video might not be admissible in trial, but it should change Shortle's mind, all right."

"And I have one other question. How hard would it be to break out of the Crab County Jail?"

"*What?*"

"Oh, nothing. We can talk about it later."

As MELLOW AND avuncular Affird may have seemed in his new incarnation, I had no desire to be alone with the vampire in his condo the following night. Instead, I met him in the card room off the lobby, which was empty. The blood bus had just pulled up outside, and all the card-playing vampires were in line, waiting for their pints.

I laid out for Affird a general timeline of the murders and Matt's connections to the victims. I told him I was surprised he hadn't heard about the homicides, which were big news in this little city.

"I don't follow the news anymore," he said. "Humans die all the time. What's the big deal? Golf news, I follow. There's no better way to pass the time aimlessly than to watch tournaments on cable TV."

"Well, no news source has covered Matt's arrest yet. I'm hoping they'll take up his cause. You know, like he's a First Amendment martyr, unfairly jailed by a corrupt police department."

"They're incompetent, not corrupt. Trust me, I used to work there."

"Well, I'm ready to go to Shortle with the video I have of the surf fisherman's confession."

I played it for Affird.

He grunted. "Well, he can't claim he didn't know you were filming him."

"Nope. And if this video doesn't make Shortle come around, I'm going to give it to *The Jellyfish Beach Journal* and local TV news."

"Do they have anything connecting Matt with the first two victims, aside from his prior reporting?"

"Just circumstantial stuff."

"Like what?" Affird asked, his eyes narrowing.

"Well, he had a verbal altercation with the first victim, Puttle, while the police were responding to a report about a shotgun blast. And he made a police report claiming Puttle fired gunshots into Matt's bungalow. Then, Matt happened to be paddleboarding in the vicinity when Puttle was drowned."

Affird nodded and chewed on his lip, his fangs showing.

"What about the second victim?" he asked. "Any circumstantial evidence linking Rosen to him?"

"Not that I know of."

"You need to feel Shortle out about this. Go to the station with Rosen's lawyer and show her the video. See how it goes from there."

"Can you come with us?"

"Nah, I don't want them to see me. It's becoming more obvious that I'm not the same Fred Affird they used to work with."

"There's one other thing," I said, explaining the odd fact that Burt Umber and Elizabeth Chubb were both at the waterfront park at the same time on the day I was following her.

"I don't know what to make of that. Could be just a coincidence. We'll need to dig deeper."

I MET Paul Leclerc in the parking lot behind the police station. His fees were still being paid by me, and they were getting significantly larger now that Matt had been arrested. But I didn't have the heart to tell Matt that he had to pay now.

"Don't be disappointed if Shortle acts uninterested in your video," Paul said. "She'll be keeping her cards close to her vest."

And, as he had predicted, the detective's expression was blank after I played the video.

"He obviously knew he was being filmed," Paul said to Shortle.

"Yes. But was he telling the truth?" she responded. "How do I know you didn't slip him some potion from your botanica? I will interview him again before I take this video too seriously."

"He puts a big dent in your case against Matt," I said.

Paul glared at me. I guess I should have let him do the lawyerly talking.

"The only witness against Matt recanted." I just couldn't keep my mouth shut.

"The state attorney and I will decide how to proceed with this case," Shortle replied.

"And you won't charge him with the murder of Charles

Chubb, I hope," I said, followed by another of Paul's disapproving stares.

"We haven't brought charges yet, but we might. That's all I can say."

"But there's nothing tying Matt to his murder. All Matt did was write articles about Chubb's arrests. You can't penalize him for his free speech."

"What makes you think that's the only evidence we have?"

"Because there's nothing else."

"Don't be so sure." Shortle smirked.

"What are you saying?" I asked. "Did you find something?"

"It would be helpful if you would tell us," Paul said.

"You know very well that it will be spelled out in the charges against him. You'll see the evidence during discovery prior to the trial."

"You're bluffing!" I said.

Now, both Shortle and Paul were frowning at me. The meeting appeared to be over. I emailed the video to Shortle before I left the building.

When we parted in the parking lot, Paul told me to be patient.

"Things will start looking better soon. Hang in there."

I thought of a few choice, sarcastic words, but I held my tongue and hugged him goodbye. He drove away in his German luxury car, and I remained seated in my deteriorating Japanese car with its jaw-dropping number on the odometer. I pondered what my next move should be to exonerate Matt.

Shortle exited the building and headed for the employees' parking lot. She hadn't noticed me. As she drove away, the thought occurred to me she might be on her way to pay a visit to Todd Oddbelly and ask him about my video.

I pulled out of my space and began following her. What I hoped to accomplish, I had no idea. I just needed to be doing something—anything.

We went a short distance west, and then south, and sure enough, we entered the neighborhood where Oddbelly lived. And sure enough, she turned onto his street and parked in front of his house.

I stopped a couple of houses down, hoping she wouldn't see my car. A wreck like mine is more memorable than a fancy new car.

From my angle, I could see that Mrs. Oddbelly's car was not there, just the large SUV parked behind the tow truck. Shortle went up to the front door, pressed the doorbell, waited, knocked on the door, and waited some more.

Either he wasn't home, or he was hiding from her in his closet.

Finally, Shortle stepped away from the door and headed back to her car.

Suddenly, she stopped and stared at the driveway. She walked over to it and went between the tow truck and the SUV, which was blocking the view of the truck from the street.

She became agitated and pulled her phone from her pocket. She dropped it on the driveway and bent down to pick it up.

I was out of my car and running toward her before my mind decided to do so.

Approaching from behind her, I saw the scene the SUV had blocked.

Oddbelly dangled from the back of the flatbed, wrapped in

the steel cable of the winch from his legs and up to and around his neck.

Clearly, he was dead. And he hadn't done this to himself, because if so, the motor of the winch would still be running. Its switch was up at the front of the flatbed, far from his reach.

Shortle turned and saw me while she was speaking on her phone to the dispatcher.

"Why are you here?" she asked me.

"Why was he killed?" I replied.

Neither question received an answer.

CHAPTER 13
MAGICAL TRACKING

"**W**ere you following me here?" Shortle demanded.

"Duh. I wanted to see if you were going to arrest Oddbelly."

"I only wanted to talk to him." She looked at his body hanging, wrapped in a steel-cable cocoon. "Too late for that."

"I don't understand why anyone would kill him. His confession was Matt's ticket to freedom. Now what?"

"You go home and let us professionals investigate."

"If there truly is a serial killer in Jellyfish Beach," I said, "it obviously can't be Matt. He's in jail and couldn't have done this."

"If Rosen is a serial killer, it doesn't mean he's responsible for every murder in town."

"But there are so few murders here. Well, that used to be the case. Is a growing murder rate a sign that Jellyfish Beach has reached the big leagues?"

Shortle shook her head defensively. "I think you should leave the crime scene."

"Don't worry. It's only a coincidence that the murder rate went up after you joined the police department."

I wasn't succeeding in making friends today.

"Even with the SUV blocking the view of the body, this murder was right out in the open," I said. "There must be a witness or two. Or it was captured on someone's security camera. Though the neighbors don't look like the type who spend oodles on stuff like that."

"I don't need you to tell me how to do my job."

A patrol car approached. No lights were flashing because there was no need to hurry.

"Okay, Detective," I said. "I'll leave you to your detecting."

While I was driving to the botanica, I called Paul and told him about the murder.

"Are you sure it wasn't an accident?" he asked.

"Pretty sure. What does this mean for Matt?"

"It's not the end of the world. There was a good chance Oddbelly would have recanted his confession, but with the focus on him now, the police can hopefully find forensic evidence connecting him to the strangulation of Jacobs. And we have the video of his confession. What I'm concerned about is if the police have anything tying Matt to the first two murders. Other than the articles he wrote under his First Amendment rights."

"Yeah. There are two individuals who need looking into."

Burt Umber had the strongest motives for killing Puttle, but he allegedly had an alibi. Elizabeth Chubb had the strongest motive for killing her abusive husband, but she, too, claimed she had an alibi. And my truth spell made her sound innocent.

The thing about the truth spell, though, was that sometimes, the enchanted subjects spoke very literally. She said she hadn't killed her husband, but I never asked her if she had convinced someone else to do it.

Someone like Burt Umber. He had bonded out after his arrest for the human smuggling much too easily. Until his future trial, he was free to create all the trouble he wanted.

The two made a very unlikely romantic couple, but they could know each other somehow. Them being inside the park convenience store at the same time gave credence to that theory.

But how could I investigate this? I didn't have the time, and it was logistically impossible for me to surveil both of them constantly.

Still, I had magic. And a vampire ex-detective.

First came the magic. I found the address of the Chubbs' home via the county property appraiser's website. This was where Elizabeth lived with her young son and daughter, and where Charles used to reside before restraining orders forced him to move to the condo where he was killed.

Unfortunately, it was a gated community, and when I saw the line of cars waiting to pass through the gate, I determined that the guard was strict in demanding permission to visit residents. I wouldn't be able to just talk my way in.

So, I turned to Affird for help. Not for his vampire powers, but his ex-detective powers. You see, Affird had neglected to turn in his badge when he "retired." He gave me a ride to the Chubbs' community after dark, and him flashing his badge was enough to get us through the gate.

Thankfully, Elizabeth's car was parked in her driveway, not in her garage. Affird pulled up at the curb, and I hopped out, making sure no one was around. Crouching behind her car, I conjured a magic ward and attached the spell to her car.

I would use the ward to track Elizabeth's car, as if I had planted a GPS device on it. It would also alert me if she approached the other wards I was about to conjure.

Next, we drove to the park in Port Inferno. Being so late, it was closed, with the gate arm padlocked shut. I installed a ward on the gate, which would alert me when the ward on Elizabeth's car approached. Next, we hopped the gate arm and walked over to the convenience store, where I installed another ward.

The marina and Umber's houseboat were on the adjacent property. Security was non-existent, so we drove in and parked a safe distance from Umber's houseboat. This was where Affird's vampire senses would come in handy.

I told him that Umber was armed and had captured us the last time we stopped by his humble abode.

"All right. Give me a few minutes," he said, getting out of the car and disappearing into the darkness.

Less than a minute later, he appeared by my window. I jumped.

"Umber's houseboat is empty," he said. "There's no car near it, and I don't sense any humans around except for a few who are living on their boats."

"Great. Thanks."

Affird drove me to the houseboat, where I conjured an additional ward to alert me if Elizabeth came here.

"I wish his car was around so I could put a ward on it," I said.

"Put one on his work boat."

I didn't know which boat in the marina was Umber's. The news reports about the murder hadn't mentioned the boat's name, because it was just a small one. But I had a semi-complicated spell that could use Umber's traces of psychic energy in his houseboat to lead me to the same energy on his work vessel.

Clutching the power charm in my pocket with one hand, I grasped his front doorknob in my other as I cast the spell. It isolated the greatest amount of psychic energy on the hardware, which would be Umber's, from anyone else's who had touched it.

I concentrated the energy into a glowing orb, which I held in my hand.

"Let's go," I said. "Be patient, because it might take a while."

As we approached the complex of finger piers that separated dozens of slips containing boats large and small, Affird elbowed me.

"Start over there." He pointed to a ramshackle dock at the edge of the marina, closer to Umber's houseboat. At this dock were several rowboats, dinghies, and small fishing skiffs that didn't warrant slips of their own.

"Good idea."

There was a beat-up skiff piled with empty crab trays that caught my eye. As I approached it, the orb of energy in my hand glowed brighter and became warmer, almost too hot to hold.

Yep, this was Umber's boat.

I conjured a new ward and attached it to the boat.

But I had one more idea. We drove to a nearby drawbridge leading to the beach. The ocean inlet and crabbing spots were in the other direction, so if Umber were taking his boat into town, he would have to pass beneath this bridge.

We parked near the bridge, and I quickly ran onto it and installed one last ward. Our night's mission was complete.

IT WAS THE NEXT DAY, and I was working at the botanica when I felt the prickling on my scalp and whistling in my ears. One of my wards had been tripped.

I was in the middle of a disagreement with a customer who planned to sacrifice chickens on her landlord's front steps as part of a Santeria curse. I tried to convince her not to kill the chickens and to substitute a potion that we sold. She wasn't buying my argument.

Finally, Luisa returned from the back room, and I thrust her into the situation. She was a Santeria priestess and had the authority that I lacked. I wished her luck. My triggered ward demanded all my attention.

I went into the back room Luisa had just left. This was where Luisa held Santeria ceremonies, Madame Tibodet had voodoo consultations, and where we offered spiritual support to any customer, no matter what religion they practiced.

This was the quiet space I needed to put myself into the meditative state that allowed me to connect with the ward.

I sensed the triggered ward was the one on Elizabeth's car.

She had just driven right by the one I'd left at the entrance to the park in Port Inferno.

"Luisa, I need to run a quick errand," I said as I rushed through the store. She was still arguing with the wannabe chicken executioner.

It seemed like I hit every red light as I sped toward Port Inferno. When I was about halfway there, another ward alerted me. I pulled into a shopping center so I could focus, and I discovered it was the ward I'd attached to Umber's houseboat. Elizabeth's car was parked beside it.

I had to find out what was going on. I couldn't imagine Elizabeth and Umber having an affair, but it would explain why she had been at the park's convenience store when he was there.

It might also suggest that Umber was involved in Charles Chubb's murder. Despite his alibi, I was still certain Umber had killed Puttle. If he was having an affair with Elizabeth, it was easy to believe she had convinced him to kill her husband or hire a lowlife thug to do it.

Just as I was driving into the marina, a car passed me on the way out. It was Elizabeth. I was too late to observe what she'd been doing.

I parked a ways back from the boat slips and, favoring the shadows, carefully approached Umber's houseboat. His pickup truck was parked nearby. I didn't dare confront him, but perhaps I could sneak up and plant a ward on his truck.

No such luck. He came out the front door, hopped in the truck, and roared away.

Dejected, I drove back to the park and wandered over to the store. The small building was packed with a weird assortment of merchandise, from fishing tackle and paddling accessories to snacks, baked goods, and coffee. Because I had previously seen Elizabeth buy a smoothie here, I ordered a berry and banana one.

The smoothie was quite good, I discovered as I strolled outside back to my car. That was when I spotted the toothless old crabber I had spoken to here before. Larry was fishing on the pier beside the boat ramp.

"Excuse me," I said, walking up to him. "I don't know if you remember me. We met the other day at the boat ramp. I'm looking for a woman named Elizabeth Chubb." I described her appearance. "She was probably here visiting Burt Umber."

Larry nodded without looking at me. "You just missed her."

His silver-streaked black hair was sun-bleached and long, pulled back in a ponytail. Studying him more closely than I had before, I realized he was probably younger than his weathered face and missing teeth suggested.

"Um, do you know why she was here?"

He finally looked at me. "Why do you care?"

I didn't know why Larry would be protective of Umber, let alone Elizabeth.

"Long story," I said. "I'm investigating her to help a friend."

Larry raised his eyebrows in a way that said, "And why?"

I decided to go for it.

"My friend is accused of murdering her husband, but I think Elizabeth had something to do with it."

Larry smiled and laughed. Though his front teeth were missing, the rest of them appeared to be present and accounted for.

"You think she got Burt to do it?" he asked.

"I don't know. Or does he know people who could have done it?"

"He knows plenty of people like that. Because of his side hustle."

"And what would that be?" I said, playing dumb.

"Crabbing and fishing aren't dependable ways to make a living. But Burt knows some people in the import business, and sometimes he makes a few bucks that way. He has a boat, after all."

"Are you talking about migrants? Or drugs?"

He shrugged and reeled in his line. "Maybe both." He checked the health of his live shrimp below a cork bobber and cast the rig perpendicular to the pier.

The situation was crystallizing in my mind.

"Was Elizabeth buying drugs from Burt?" I asked.

"I'm not a narc. You can draw your own conclusions."

"I'm not sure how to put this. Elizabeth travels in very different circles than Burt Umber. How did she meet him?"

"Mutual friends from way back when they all, you know, partied maybe a bit too hard. The friends hooked Elizabeth up with Burt."

So, Elizabeth *was* buying drugs from Umber. That's why she came down here to the park.

"Please, I need to know," I implored him. "Did Umber kill Charles Chubb?"

"I don't know. And if I did, I wouldn't tell anyone except the police, and only if they had me in an interrogation room. But I know Burt well enough. If he ever killed anyone, it would be because of passion, not for hire."

"Was he involved romantically with Elizabeth?"

"I wouldn't know. I do know Burt has a Cuban chica he sees every weekend."

"So, you think he referred Elizabeth to someone who could do the job?"

He shrugged again. "I told you he knows people like that."

"One last question. Do you think Burt killed Jerome Puttle?"

He laughed. "I did at first. But he says he was down at the Seminole casino at the time, and he has people who can back him up. I guess someone else killed that stupid bully, Puttle."

It was obvious I wouldn't get any more valuable information from Larry, so I thanked him and headed back to Jellyfish Beach.

Later that night, when I was home, a tingling and whistling told me another ward had been triggered. I opened my mind to the magic.

The ward was the one I'd left on the bridge. It had been set off by the ward I had put on Burt's boat.

Burt was cruising toward downtown Port Inferno at a very odd hour for boating.

CHAPTER 14
CHEZ CARRASCAL

Burt Umber's skiff was headed up Stingray Creek, the tidal river that ran past the fishing village of Port Inferno and emptied into the Intracoastal Waterway near the inlet. I couldn't follow him without a boat, but I assumed he would moor somewhere in or near town.

The spell I had used to create the wards enabled me to home in on the one I'd attached to his boat. As I drove toward Port Inferno, I could sense only his general location on the river nearing the town. When I arrived, I parked in a small waterfront park in the business district where I could clear my mind and focus on the ward.

This park was nothing like the sprawling one downriver next to the marina where Umber lived. This park was small and tidy with a gazebo. It felt safe here, despite the late hour.

And despite whatever nefarious activity Burt was up to.

Focusing on the ward while clutching my power charm, I

became one with the ward. My senses were transported to the bow of Umber's skiff where I had attached the magic.

I was there amid the slapping of water against the hull, the rumble of the outboard engine, the rich salty breeze tinged with the gasoline-oil exhaust. The boat was nearing the town from the south of where I had parked.

There was only a sliver of a moon in the starry sky, providing little illumination, yet Umber piloted the boat without his running lights on. He must know these waters well. And he was undoubtedly running dark because he was up to no good.

Through my psychic connection to the ward, I could see he was headed to the waterfront restaurant called Crabby's. Normally, I would assume he was bringing freshly harvested crabs to sell. But not at this late hour. And not while running dark.

I drove to the closed restaurant but didn't park there. Instead, I left my car outside of a neighboring home that had been converted to a high-end gift shop. Passing between the two properties, I reached the river and hid behind a fence in the former home's backyard. I could peer around the end of the fence to see the restaurant.

Soon, Umber's boat came into view, riding low in the water as if it carried a heavy load. Umber sat astern with one hand on the engine's tiller behind him.

Was he carrying drugs? That would be my bet. His boat was too small to travel offshore to meet ships in international waters. But he could ferry drugs from boats that had come into the inlet.

I didn't know who owned Crabby's, but it would surprise

me if they were involved in the drug trade. Why would they risk their restaurant business by allowing the narcotics to pass through the property?

Turns out they didn't. Umber's boat kept going past the restaurant and the yard of the shop where I was hiding, finally pulling up to the dock of a private home next to the shop.

After he had passed me, I crept along the waterfront until I reached the fence between the shop and the private home. I had a good view of Umber tying off his boat and handing small wooden crates to two men who had appeared at the end of the dock.

The crates didn't look like they would hold drugs. They looked like the kind you'd pack with crabs or oysters. That was why they were used.

A more complete picture of Umber was forming in my mind. Crabbing was his day job, but what really brought the cash in was the drug trade. When he wasn't smuggling migrants. And on top of all this, he was a small-time drug dealer who sold drugs to suburbanites like Elizabeth Chubb.

Was he who murdered Charles Chubb? Was it over drug money?

Yet, Umber's ambitions were greater than small-time dealing. He was running drugs, too. Perhaps, that's why he killed Puttle. It hadn't been a petty dispute over stolen crabs; Puttle knew about Umber's smuggling and threatened to turn him in.

Of course, I was wildly speculating. It's what you do when you're crouching beside a fence in the dark with dangerous men within shouting distance of you.

But I wouldn't be surprised if my theories were at least partially right. Except, I didn't know where Oddbelly fit in.

Maybe, when he was fishing, he saw some things he wasn't supposed to see. Or, he sold some of the drugs Umber smuggled in and had died over a money dispute or a double cross.

All this speculating was entertaining enough, but how would I prove any of it? That was beyond my powers as a witch/amateur sleuth, even if I could use my truth spell.

It looked as though all the crates had been unloaded from Umber's boat. He fired up his outboard and sped past me in the direction from which he had come.

Did he glance in my direction? It seemed like it.

No, I was just being paranoid. I stood up and crept away from the water, staying close to the fence so the guys on the other side wouldn't see me.

"Are you a cop?" a man in a hoodie asked at the end of the fence near the street.

He aimed a pistol at me. So much for my efforts at staying unseen.

"No," I said as calmly as my racing heart would allow. "I'm a witch."

My sleep spell is quick to cast, thank goodness. The gunman dropped to the yard, snoring.

I sprinted toward the street until my head snapped violently backward as someone grabbed my long hair, yanking me to the ground.

A sweatshirt was wrapped around my face, blinding me. It smelled like it had been sweated in for years by a man who ate spicy foods and never washed himself or the sweatshirt.

"Tie her hands," said a voice near my head. "Help me carry her to the car."

"What about Ramon?" asked another voice.

"He'll wake up when he's done with his nap."

They didn't know it, but I couldn't cast a sleeping spell on them because I needed to see them to do so. The same applied to my immobility spell. There were other spells I could cast while blinded, but, frankly, I was panicking too much to concentrate.

I was certain they were going to kill me and dump my body somewhere.

Finally, my brain thought of a strategy.

"Felix Carrascal is my friend," I said, my voice muffled by the stinky sweatshirt. "He'll be angry if you hurt me."

"She knows Carrascal?"

"She's lying."

"What if she isn't?"

"Bring me to Mr. Carrascal," I said. "You'll see that he knows me. I was his guest once in his beachfront mansion. He showed me his kazoo collection."

"Ah, the beautiful kazoos."

Hands under my armpits lifted me to my feet. Each man took an arm and led me quickly across the grass, then across a paved surface. A car door opened, and I was shoved inside onto a bench seat. One man sat beside me. I heard the other one get into the front seat.

"Are we taking her to Carrascal?" the one beside me asked.

"Yes. The van with the product has left. Our job here is done, except to deal with her. If she's lying, we'll kill her at the beach."

As the car pulled away, music came over the stereo—a mega-famous female artist.

"Her new album is so beautiful," said the man beside me in a choked-up voice. "Her lyrics truly are poetry. Whenever I hear her songs, I question my career."

"Really? Why?"

"Don't get me wrong. Smuggling drugs and killing people pays the bills and gives me something to do. But her music makes me feel that there are loftier things to live for."

"You mean, getting beautiful women like her?"

"No. Expressing my soul with music like she does. Don't tell anyone, but I've been taking kazoo lessons from Mr. Carrascal. He says I'm a natural."

"Anyone can play the kazoo."

"Anyone can make noise. Only a master can play beautiful music. Someday, I want to be like Mr. Carrascal."

"You mean, rich?"

"No. A master musician. Bringing happiness to people through my music. Music like this, except played with kazoos."

"You have too soft a heart to be in this business. Maybe I should kill you after we kill this lady."

"Wait until I have mastered the kazoo. It will be the highest point of my life. Then, you can kill me."

When the car stopped, the guy next to me pulled me out. I still had the noxious sweatshirt wrapped around my head.

"Can you remove this from my face?" I asked. "Mr. Carrascal will be offended by the smell."

Only one guy laughed.

"I've been to his mansion before. There's no reason to blindfold me."

But when the sweatshirt was taken away, I saw we weren't

at the mansion. We were in front of a smaller beachfront home. By smaller, I mean it was probably worth eight figures instead of nine.

"Oh. He got a new house?" I asked.

"He still has the mansion, but the Feds are always staking it out." I recognized the voice as being the man who had sat in the back seat with me. The kazoo musician in training. He was short and stocky with beefy hands. But you didn't need delicate fingers to play the kazoo.

"Wait here," ordered the other man, who was taller and had crude prison tattoos on his face and hands.

"Your passion for the kazoo is very inspiring," I said to my guard as we stood in the stone portico of the mansion.

He smiled. "To put a bullet in someone's heart is easy. To fill that heart with beauty is worth so much more."

"I'm glad you feel that way. No need for any bullets with me."

A man I recognized as a bodyguard came out the front door and scanned me with a metal detector. Next, he patted me down.

"What's in the left pocket of your jeans?" he asked.

"It's just a monkey's paw in a pouch with some herbs and lizard skin."

He stepped away from me with distaste. "You can go inside."

I entered the two-story-tall foyer with marble covering both the floor and walls.

A housekeeper in a black uniform appeared out of nowhere and greeted me.

"Please follow me to the parlor," she said. "You can wait for the boss there."

The parlor was to our left. It had a fireplace and high-backed chairs. Along one wall was a carved oak table covered with trays of cookies and hors d'oeuvres. Bottles of high-end water were at the end.

"When we're not expecting visitors, we use this as our break room," she explained before disappearing.

I checked out the food on the table. My stomach growled, but I felt weird helping myself, considering the circumstances.

Suddenly, a man was beside me, filling a plate with egg rolls, shrimp, roast-beef sliders, and deviled eggs.

"You should try the deviled eggs," he said in a slight Spanish accent. "And the macaroons. Sinfully good."

His voice was slightly muffled, and I looked up at him. He wore a balaclava that covered his entire head and face, except for his eyes, which were hidden behind mirrored sunglasses.

"Thank you," I said. "I will in a little while."

I stepped aside to give him room to load his plate.

"Are you a friend or family of Mr. Carrascal?" he asked.

"A friend," I replied. "Are you, too?"

"No, I work here. I'm the torturer."

"Oh. I didn't know that was a career path anymore."

"It sure is. Many drug lords outsource their torturers, but Mr. Carrascal is truly old school. He likes all his talent to work in-house."

"That's good to know."

He lifted the bottom of his balaclava to gain access to his mouth, into which he stuffed a deviled egg.

"Have you been, um, particularly busy?" I asked.

"It's been slow this week. But you know how it is. One moment, you're bored, and the next, you're too busy to even take a break. You're like, where did the day go?"

"I'm sure your prisoners don't feel that way."

He laughed. "Not if I'm doing my job right."

I was getting really worried that I would become part of his job, but just then, Felix Carrascal bounded into the room wearing a swimsuit and T-shirt.

He was short and rotund, with fake-looking black hair. Since I'd last seen him, he'd shaved off his beard and left a small black mustache, dyed black, and waxed to curve upward in tiny points. It made him look like Hercule Poirot.

His bodyguard followed him into the room and stationed himself in the corner, watching me suspiciously. There would be no chance of me sprinkling truth-spell powder on his boss's feet.

"What a delight to have you visit me again," Carrascal said, giving me a kiss on the cheek.

"Good to see you, too, sir. I love your new home."

"This is just a cottage compared to my mansion. But the DEA is always surveilling that place. I've decided to convert it into a museum."

"Oh, good! You said you've always wanted a kazoo museum."

"Yes. Technically, it will be a museum about me, with an emphasis on kazoos."

"That's wonderful. Most people need to be dead to have a museum dedicated to them."

Wrong thing to say. Carrascal stiffened and looked over his

shoulder. The torturer placed his hand on the butt of a pistol protruding from beneath his shirt.

"But let us not talk about gloomy topics," Carrascal said, brightening again. "I understand you were spying on one of my business operations this evening."

"No. I mean, yes, but I hadn't known it was yours. I was lucky it was, I guess. You see, I was following a crabber and low-level drug dealer who I believe is a murderer."

I went on to explain the complicated story of the four murders, and how Matt was in jail, suspected in three of them.

"I remember your friend," Carrascal said. "He wrote a splendid story about my kazoo collection. For that, I am grateful. Who is this crabber you speak of?"

"His name is Burt Umber."

"Shall I dispose of him?"

"No. No, please don't. I want to prove he's guilty of the murders and for the police to arrest him."

Carrascal nodded. And gobbled down a deviled egg.

"Excuse me, sir and madam, I must go back to work now," the torturer said, heading for the door. "I don't want to keep my clients waiting."

After the torturer left, I asked Carrascal to tell his men not to be alarmed if they saw me following Umber during drug runs.

"I'll put out the word, but I recommend you stay clear of my operations," Carrascal said, devouring another egg. He didn't seem interested in my story anymore.

"I blame Detective Shortle of the Jellyfish Beach Police Department for railroading Matt," I said.

Carrascal perked up. "Shortle, you say?"

"She doesn't have any actual evidence tying him to the crimes," I said. "She has some crazy theory that he's a crusading reporter killing these men out of moral outrage."

"You speak of crusading? That describes the detective. She has been a pest to me ever since she began working in this town. So naïve and inexperienced. She thought it would boost her career to take down the city's wealthiest businessman, but she has no idea what she's doing or how dangerous it is."

His outburst piqued my interest. "Do you think she'd cross the line to take you down?" I asked. "Do you think she's a dirty cop?"

"I think she would cross the line. She's a fanatic. Where I grew up, cops like her are common. But it's also common for them to get killed."

"Oh my. I wonder if she would cross the line in other ways."

"What do you mean?"

"Kill bad men without putting them through the justice system."

Carrascal cocked his head. "You know, she very well could do that. The fanatic that she is."

"I would like to investigate her, too. I mean, if you release me."

"As long as you don't report what you saw on the waterfront this evening, you are free to go. My men will give you a ride to your car."

"Thank you, sir!"

"Take some deviled eggs with you."

Of course, nothing would stop me from reporting Burt Umber's involvement in the drug smuggling. However, there was no need to mention Carrascal, since everyone from the local police to the Feds knew what he was up to.

Yet now my ire was directed at Shortle, like a missile changing course in mid-flight.

As I exited the mini mansion, the notes of *The Godfather* theme song drifted into the foyer. Played on a kazoo, of course.

CHAPTER 15

INTERROGATE THE INTERROGATOR

"Good evening, Detective," I said when Affird answered his phone. Despite being retired, he preferred to be addressed that way.

"What can I do for you, Ms. Mindle?" His gruff, flat voice displayed the tiniest bit of pleasure to hear from me.

I didn't want to mention Carrascal, but I did describe what Umber was up to the previous night. I explained how drugs could connect the murders that put Matt in jail.

"But I also thought of a more far-fetched theory I wanted to bounce off you. What if Shortle has gone rogue?"

"In what way?"

"What if she extrajudicially executed those men?"

Affird didn't reply. Maybe I shouldn't have brought this up. After all, Affird was known to execute supernaturals back in the day.

Finally, he laughed. "Yeah, right. Why would she do that?"

"It's the exact same thing she's accusing Matt of doing. It's no more unlikely that she could do it. She's so self-righteous, after all. I could believe she'd take out a domestic abuser and a guy who fires a shotgun next to his kid's bed. Do you know anything about her that would support this theory?"

"No. Well, there was a story about her when she was a uniformed cop, fresh out of the academy. She caught a guy who mugged an old lady and broke a couple of her bones. When he resisted arrest, Shortle almost beat him to death with her nightstick."

"See, that's exactly the kind of thing I'm talking about. If she's capable of that, who says she couldn't go even further?"

"Very unlikely. She's matured since then."

"That's what you want to believe."

"Listen, I'm not saying cops have never killed people for the wrong reasons. But what's in it for her to execute those guys? Why risk her career and her freedom when we have a justice system to punish them?"

I had to admit, my theory seemed a bit over the top.

"I guess you're right," I said.

"I thought you and Shortle were getting along, after a fashion. You were helping her with the occult stuff."

"She went too far when she arrested Matt. I don't trust her anymore."

"She probably has evidence you don't know about."

"Yeah." I recalled Shortle alluding to that fact.

"Give her some slack," Affird said. "Your theory about the drug connections is a lot more believable."

"Do you think she'd listen if I told her about the drug theory?"

"I don't know. But it's worth a try."

So, can you believe I invited Shortle to lunch? Yeah, the woman who arrested Matt—I asked her to meet me at the Jellyfish Beach Diner.

Predictably, she turned me down. However, she met with me at the police department, in a large, windowless conference room with a video monitor mounted to the wall, along with the most vapid motivational posters.

"I have some information you might want," I said. "If you don't have it already."

"Go ahead," she replied, with a notepad on the table in front of her and a digital audio recorder running. "I'm meeting with you in good faith."

My intentions weren't entirely in good faith. But what could I do? My friend, and potential love interest, was rotting in jail. And my mother wanted me to break him out, endangering my life, liberty, and pursuit of witchiness.

"I'll skip the small talk and get right to the point," I said. "Are you aware that Burt Umber runs drugs ashore and is also a small-time dealer?"

Shortle frowned and scribbled on her pad. "We had suspicions about him being a dealer. But not about running drugs. Tell me more."

I recounted the events of the other night when I witnessed him offloading drugs. Left out, of course, was any mention of magical wards or Felix Carrascal.

"How can you be certain there were drugs in those crates and not oysters or something?"

I wished I could mention Carrascal. But I had promised him

I wouldn't. And it's not wise to break a promise with a drug lord.

"He traveled at night with no running lights on his boat. The dock where he delivered the goods had no lights on. And the men who took the goods were heavily armed."

"Okay." She wrote something. "Anything else?"

I gave a jumbled summary of my investigations, including him being visited by Elizabeth Chubb, who, according to Larry, was buying drugs from him.

"Couldn't drugs tie the murders together?" I asked. "Maybe Charles Chubb owed lots of money to Umber for drugs, and Umber killed him. Maybe Puttle witnessed Umber transferring drugs from a larger boat, so Umber killed him."

"What about the two shark fishermen?"

"I already told you Oddbelly confessed to strangling Jacobs on the beach. It could be that he himself was killed because of drug-related debts. Or, he witnessed Umber picking up drugs from a boat offshore."

"You've given me a lot of maybes," Shortle said. "Too many maybes to count."

"I'm just connecting the dots. If you want to connect them differently, go ahead. I'm not a detective."

"Precisely. I thank you, though, for the information."

Her attitude was a little too smug. My bad-faith intentions rose to the surface.

And I cast the truth spell. Tossing the powder at her feet beneath the table was super awkward, since the table was too wide.

"Is something wrong?" Shortle asked.

"I think a mosquito was biting me."

Her eyes got the familiar glassy look, but she appeared to be fighting the urge to talk. Shortle was a very disciplined person with strong self-control.

"Tell me, honestly," I said, "do you believe Matt committed the murders?"

She tried, but failed to resist. "Not really."

Aha!

"But," she continued, "the state attorney is still interested in him. There's evidence we can't just ignore."

"Like what?"

She tried to stay silent, but her lips moved anyway. "Surveillance footage."

"Of what?"

"Of Rosen's car near the Chubb murder scene."

"What do you mean by 'near'?"

"It passed by Chubb's condo on Highway A1A shortly after the time of death."

"Oh, come on! A1A is a major road. Dozens, or hundreds, of cars passed by around that same time."

"There's more," Shortle said, struggling not to speak. "The crystal statuette that bludgeoned the victim had partial prints from Rosen on it."

"No way!"

"Under interrogation, Rosen claimed he touched the statuette when he was in the condo months ago, arriving with the police after Mrs. Chubb reported a violation of the restraining order. The prints looked as though he tried to wipe them away. Or someone wearing gloves handled the sculpture more recently. Oh, why am I telling you this?"

"Don't be so hard on yourself," I said. Though I really meant, *Stop fighting my spell*.

"You can see why it's difficult to drop the charges on Rosen just yet, even though I'm not a hundred percent sure he's guilty. Remember how belligerent he was with the first victim? And he accused the victim of shooting at his home. The police who were with him in Chubb's condo reported his belligerence to that victim, too. And he readily admits he confronted the third victim, even though someone else confessed to that murder. Along with all of this, there are thousands of words of newspaper copy he wrote that are almost Old Testament in their scathing condemnations."

"Free speech," I said, though I didn't sound confident.

"Matt Rosen had strong motives to kill those men."

"Tell me, Detective. How do you feel about those men?"

Her eyes burned with intensity, but she fought the urge to open up to me.

"They were evil," she replied in a terse voice.

"Isn't the world better off without them?"

She nodded but stopped herself. "It's not for me to judge that."

This woman, one of the biggest control freaks I have ever known, continued to fight my spell. And she was winning.

"Do you believe some people don't deserve the presumption of innocence?" I asked. "That the justice system is more than they deserve?"

"I investigate crimes and make arrests. It's not my place to be the judge or jury."

"Admit it—those men got what was coming to them."

She shook her head. "I can't."

"Maybe if you took out those men yourself, it wouldn't have been such a bad thing."

She shook her head, struggling.

"That's what you did? Right?"

"I couldn't..."

"You couldn't let them live?"

"I couldn't do what you're suggesting. No, I couldn't."

The truth spell was wearing off, mostly because of her superhuman resistance to it. I could give it some more energy, but I would feel bad prolonging her agony.

She wouldn't admit to killing them, but that didn't mean she didn't do it. Deciphering the tortured expressions on her face and her labored breathing, though, I would put my money on her not killing them.

Yet, she left me with no doubt that she had at least considered it.

I thanked her and left the conference room. My last view was a poster on the wall with a photo of a man on a mountain peak that said: "The higher you go, you better not fall."

At this point, I still believed my theory that Umber was the strongest suspect. It seemed a little too easy, but it was the most logical. I had no clue of how I could prove it, aside from putting Umber under the truth spell, and he would never give me the opportunity.

Meanwhile, I couldn't stop thinking about Matt's prints on the crystal statuette. His explanation for them sounded too convenient.

Did I believe him?

I would be put to the test when he called me the following night from the jail.

IN SPRITE OF HERSELF

"Yes, I accept," I told the automated female voice that greeted me when I answered the phone.

"Missy, it's me," Matt said.

"I know. There aren't any other inmates who call me."

"Have you gotten any leads that can help me?"

I gave him the long story of my surveillance of Umber and my visit to Carrascal. Matt was pleased that Carrascal appreciated the article about his kazoo collection. Don't we all crave the approval of major drug lords?

"Umber is probably the key," I said. "All the murders could be because the victims witnessed or knew about him smuggling drugs."

"Do you realize that puts you in his crosshairs? It sounds like he was the one who saw you spying on the drug transfer the other night and reported you to Carrascal's men. You need to be more careful moving forward."

The implication that I could be the next murder victim sank in, chilling me. Matt's voice snapped me out of it.

"Hello? Are you still there?"

"Yeah, yeah. I'm here. I should also mention I cast my truth spell on Shortle."

"You did? Wow."

"I wanted to feel her out, to see if she's a rogue cop who extrajudicially executed the scum of the earth—basically, what she's accusing you of doing."

"What did she say?"

"She's strong-willed and struggled against the spell. It sounded like the idea of ridding the earth of those men was tempting, but that she didn't do it. But I can't be sure."

"It's kind of hard to believe," Matt said.

153

"Three minutes remain in your account," the automated voice said. I had recently enrolled in a pre-paid service for Matt to use when calling me. It was ridiculously expensive.

"It *is* hard to believe. I also asked Shortle if she thought you were guilty."

"And?"

"She said she didn't but couldn't let you go yet. The State Attorney doesn't want to drop the charges yet, either. They have evidence I didn't realize. Like video of your car passing by Chubb's condo around the time of his murder. And what's really bothering me is your fingerprints being on the crystal statuette that killed him."

"Oh, those. I told Shortle I examined it when I was there months ago. The police had gone there to question him about violating his restraining order. I heard the call dispatching them there on my police scanner and showed up. The police didn't kick me out."

"Matt, do you realize how bad it looks to have your prints on it? Why were you touching stuff in his condo?"

"It was unusual. A crystal statuette of Venus de Milo. Kind of ironic to think he got his head bashed in by a mythological woman."

"Thirty seconds remaining," said the robot lady.

"Yeah, and you touched the stupid thing."

"It was an unfortunate coincidence."

"One that could convict you."

"Wait, you sound almost as if you're having doubts about me."

"I'm only saying—"

Click. The line went dead.

Guilt swept over me. Because I realized I really was having doubts about Matt, and that was a horrible thing to realize. My doubts felt like a betrayal of him. And a blow against our budding relationship.

I must be a bad person to allow the slightest bit of suspicion to sneak in about my friend, right?

Or maybe, I was just wary of letting a man into my heart and getting hurt again.

Was I being paranoid, or just careful?

My night was spent sleeping only occasionally, between competing bouts of guilt for doubting Matt and reassurances that it was okay to feel the way I did.

In the morning, I got up for work feeling grumpy. But I was also more determined than ever to find evidence linking Umber to the murders and exonerating Matt.

I surprised myself by how far I was willing to go.

CHAPTER 16
KIND OF A JERK

Have you ever attended a stranger's funeral, where you asked attendees for dirt on their departed loved one?

I didn't think so. But that's how I spent an otherwise lovely Friday morning, after I read in the paper the time and place of Charles Chubb's service. It was held at the local franchise of the Discount Funeral Emporium chain.

To prove my theory that Chubb had had drug connections with Umber, I needed to find actual evidence of them. Another attempt to reach out to his ex-wife had ended badly; she didn't want to talk to me anymore. So, I would have to ferret out information about a guy I didn't know at all.

He was a stockbroker, a father, and an abusive husband. He had lived in a rental condo on the beach where he'd been murdered. These facts were the extent of my knowledge.

Speaking to his neighbors at the condo complex had been a waste of time. Most didn't know him; the rest said he was quiet and unfriendly. No one knew anything about drug dealers.

So, here I was before the service began, trying to mingle with the mourners while the guy lay in a closed casket. And there weren't many to mingle with.

"Not to speak ill of the dead, but Chuck was kind of a jerk," said an elderly bald guy in a black suit. "All he cared about was being the top performer at the brokerage. He considered all of us competitors, never friends."

"I see," I replied. "Was he, by any chance, a serious drug addict?"

"I beg your pardon?"

"Or was he just into recreational drugs?"

"I wouldn't know. I don't think so."

The ex-coworker extricated himself from me very quickly after that.

Elizabeth Chubb was not here, but I spotted a young woman sitting by herself, crying. She was the only one in this sparse crowd who outwardly displayed grief.

I sat on the folding chair beside her—the uncomfortable chairs were reminders this was the Discount Funeral Emporium.

"My condolences," I said to her. "Are you a member of Charles's family?"

"I was his girlfriend," she replied, dabbing her tears.

"I'm sorry for your loss. Charles was a great man. Larger than life."

She looked at me strangely. "Are you a coworker?"

"I'm a friend of a friend. But I've been to some of his parties. Wow, they were wild!"

"How so?"

"He served several varieties of party favors, if you know what I mean."

"I don't know what you mean. I hope you're not implying something about drugs. Charles never touched them."

"These parties were long ago, probably before you began seeing him."

"We've been seeing each other for eight years."

I realized I was terrible at soliciting information from strangers. Besmirching his memory, even if he was a bad guy, was not fair to this woman.

"Are we speaking about the same man?" I asked. "Charles Mankiewicz?"

"No. My boyfriend was Charles Chubb."

"Oh my goodness! I came to the wrong funeral!" I gave a fake laugh. "So sorry for bothering you."

How foolish of me to think I could find out about someone's drug habits at his funeral? Without going right to the source—to his alleged drug dealer, Umber—I would need to spend countless hours investigating this. It was something a reporter, like Matt, or a detective, like Shortle, was trained to do.

I was merely an amateur, without the right skills and with none of the required patience.

Still, I stuck around for the service. It was presided over by the funeral director, who clearly hadn't known Charles. One person stepped up to give a short eulogy. She identified herself as his sister, a stout woman with intense eyes. The only thing she said that stood out for me was a reference to Charles "battling demons."

She could have been referring to his violent tendencies, but maybe there was more. I went along to the burial, hoping I could get a few words with her there. It was at the Jellyfish Beach Municipal Cemetery and Mausoleum.

The cemetery was like a field of memory landmines for me. Not that I had any relatives interred here, but I'd had several experiences among these graves, both pleasant and horrifying. For instance, two vampire clients held their wedding reception at the cemetery late one night. And I also fought flesh-eating ghouls who had been living underground here. So, you could say the place gave me mixed emotions.

There was no service per se at the Chubb burial. The event was all about getting the coffin from the hearse to the grave, where the funeral director said a few generic words before the few attendees drifted away.

Except for me, who made a beeline to Chubb's sister.

After the obligatory expressions of sympathy, I went right for the target.

"I apologize for being so direct, but you mentioned that Charles battled demons," I said to her.

She stared at me without surprise or any emotion.

"I know Elizabeth dabbles in substance abuse," I continued. "Did Charles suffer from that disorder, as well?"

"No. He was a violent man with violent moods and no control over them. And Elizabeth set them off regularly."

Was she trying to blame Elizabeth for the physical abuse?

"You can't blame her for getting physically attacked," I said as politely as possible.

"I'm not. But you mentioned drugs, and Liz was having an affair with her drug dealer—still is, as far as I know. Charles had no excuse for laying a hand on her, but I believe that drugs have pernicious effects, even on those who don't take them."

"I'm sorry," I said, feeling dirty. "I hope Charles's murderer is caught and convicted."

"I wouldn't be surprised if it was the drug dealer. Charles had at least one fistfight with him."

"Are the police aware of that?"

"I don't know. They never spoke to me. And I can't be sure that Elizabeth would have told them. She wouldn't want her druggie boyfriend to be a suspect, would she?"

I CHALKED this revelation up to luck, not skill. It was a big step forward in tying Umber to Chubb's murder instead of Matt. I was guilty of playing stereotypes and not seriously considering that Elizabeth and Umber could be anything more than customer and dealer, but I'm glad the sister taught me the error of my preconceptions.

"Hey, Detective, I've got some info for you," I said, surprised that Shortle took my call.

"Go ahead."

"Elizabeth Chubb is having an affair with Umber. Charles's sister told me about it. And it sounds like Elizabeth's drug use —with drugs she got from Umber—contributed to the marital strife in the Chubb household. The sister said that Chubb and Umber had a fistfight. And I could totally see Umber paying a visit to Charles Chubb on the night of his murder and arguing—"

"No. No. I'm shutting this down," Shortle said angrily. "You will *not* contact Burt Umber, and you will *not* go around asking questions about him."

"Why are you trying to protect him?"

"He's involved in more than one police investigation, and I don't want you interfering."

"You can't stop me from talking about him."

"Yes, I can. It's time for you to butt out of our investigations. You're going to do more harm than good."

"I've learned a lot of things you didn't know."

"I don't care. We've got it under control now, so please stand down."

"You still have Matt Rosen behind bars, and he's innocent."

"If he really is, his charges will be dropped."

"*If* he is? You know he's innocent."

"I'm handling this by the book. I've been patient with you for too long, Ms. Mindle, and now I'm done. Stay away from Burt Umber and stop playing amateur detective."

She ended the call. I was furious. Aside from her patronizing tone, what made me mad was the fact that Matt was still in jail, and Shortle didn't seem to want to do anything about it.

So, was I going to stop investigating? No.

In fact, I wanted to find a connection between Umber and the shark fishermen. It seemed like a stretch, but at least they were from adjacent worlds: recreational and commercial fishing.

I had a few theories about the two fishermen's deaths. The first two presumed that Oddbelly's confession was true, and he killed Billy Lee Jacobs. If we are to believe that, then, maybe someone who knew Jacobs killed Oddbelly out of revenge. If the revenge angle didn't play out, maybe Oddbelly was killed because of a dispute I knew nothing about. Another possibility, if the confession was true, was that Umber killed Oddbelly for a reason involving drugs. For instance, Oddbelly witnessed Umber smuggling drugs.

If Oddbelly had lied in his confession, despite my truth spell, maybe Umber killed both of them.

I was leaning toward the theories that pointed to Umber, which was what I hoped to prove, tying all the murders together neatly with a bow.

However, I didn't know how to proceed. Since I couldn't get advice from Matt until his next phone call, I had to turn to my vampire ex-cop.

"How confident are you in the efficacy of your truth spell?" Affird asked me, as we sat near the pool at Squid Tower.

Having been turned in his early fifties, he was younger in body age than most of the male vampires of the community. That meant he got a lot of attention from the ladies. Watching them show off their deathly pale bodies in bathing suits was one of his few pleasures as a vampire.

"The spell doesn't always work," I replied. "Some supernaturals can defeat it. Humans with strong wills and sharp minds, like Shortle, can resist it to some degree. A moron like Oddbelly? He would have no defense against the spell."

"Okay. His confession explains why the first fisherman was garroted with fishing line. You know what bothers me?"

"What?"

"Why did this Oddbelly get strangled with the cable from his truck's winch? It sounds symbolic, like someone was trying to send a message. A narco like Umber would have just shot the guy. Quick and easy and no playing around with a winch."

Affird had a point there.

"No one was shot," I said. "All the victims were killed by crude, physical means."

Affird nodded and simply stared at me through his shades, though it was a dark, moonless night.

"The question is why," he said, "when everyone owns a gun nowadays. I can see Umber killing Chubb with the crystal statuette, though, if he was there for a discussion that got out of hand, and he wasn't there intending to execute Chubb."

"An argument about Elizabeth."

"Yeah. That brings me back to the winch cable that strangled Oddbelly. It could be revenge for strangling the first fisherman."

"That's what I was thinking. But Oddbelly was blaming it on Matt. How would a friend or family member of Jacobs know Oddbelly did it?"

"Your truth spell isn't the only thing that gets people to shoot off their mouths. Beer can also have that effect. Oddbelly told someone what he did, and word got back to friends of Jacobs."

"That's a reasonable explanation," I said. "Unless Oddbelly was killed by a rival tow-truck driver. Or someone furious that Oddbelly towed their car."

"In police work, we start with the most plausible explanation first. Only if it doesn't pan out do we move on to the crazy."

"That means I need to immerse myself in the world of Billy Lee Jacobs. I'm not looking forward to that. Can you ask a former coworker to check out the arrest records of Jacobs and his family?"

"Yeah. Glasbag would do it for me. You know, you don't have to go to all this trouble investigating who killed Oddbelly. Rosen is a suspect only for Jacobs' murder. And there's only circumstantial evidence that's flimsy."

"I know. But if I can prove that Umber was involved, it would destroy their case against Matt."

I didn't mention that Shortle had ordered me to forget about Umber.

"Suit yourself," Affird said. "I'll let you know if Glasbag finds any records."

I DIDN'T KNOW how to find out if Oddbelly had been threatened by owners of cars he'd towed. He had appeared to be a one-man business. I'd have to ask his wife, but I couldn't stomach that kind of melodrama right now.

As to the theory of Oddbelly being murdered to avenge the death of Jacobs, I didn't know where to begin. I would wait until I heard if any of his relatives had been convicted of a violent felony.

What I could do right now was to ask around to see if the two shark fishermen knew Umber. My first stop in the morning was the bait shop nearest to where they had been fishing.

"Bite Me" was the uninspired name of the store. It was crammed with rods, reels, and terminal tackle, along with nets, bait buckets, and every accessory you could think of. In the rear were large tanks holding live shrimp, mullet, and minnows.

A sign on the door said the place was family owned and operated. The old man behind the counter, who I guessed was the owner, looked like he would know what fish were biting where and on what bait.

Hopefully, he knew as much about fishermen as he did about fish.

"Why are you asking about Jacobs and Oddbelly?" he demanded suspiciously.

"I'm a friend of Matt Rosen, and—"

"Oh, Matt! He's been a customer of ours for years. Dang shame he was arrested. I can't believe he murdered Jacobs and Puttle, though they weren't exactly beloved."

"He didn't murder them. I'm trying to help get him released by finding out who did."

"Good. I didn't think he did. How can I help?"

"Well, is there anyone else you think murdered them?"

"No." He scratched his brush-bristle hair. "Like I said, they weren't popular guys, but I've never heard of anyone who wanted to kill them. I'd even venture to guess that Oddbelly could have killed Jacobs. I heard they fought a lot, especially after drinking."

Little did he know how correct his instincts were.

"Do you know a commercial crabber and fisherman named Burt Umber?"

"Yeah, I know him," the owner said. "I sell him dead shrimp and mullet for him to bait his traps with. Sometimes, he buys fishing gear here."

"Did Umber know Oddbelly and Jacobs?"

"Hm, don't know." He scratched his head again. "If I had to bet, I would say yes. This is a small community, and the hardcore sportsmen's community is even smaller."

"You've never heard about Umber feuding with them or anything?"

"Nope. Why? You think Umber killed them?"

"Of course not," I lied. "But let me know if you hear of any juicy gossip about the three of them. I'll stop by again soon."

As a gesture of good will, I bought an overpriced bottle of juice. It was the only thing in the store I had any use for—and that didn't smell like fish.

I spent the rest of my day working at my actual job in the botanica. When I left for the evening, I had a flurry of errands— pharmacy, groceries, and other things that had been neglected while I spent so much time sleuthing. Then, I raced home to feed two cats and one iguana before their human could even think of feeding herself.

I was in such a rush, I barely noticed the car with its lights off parked across the street from my house, or if anyone was inside it.

Big mistake.

CHAPTER 17
EVIL HAS ENTERED THE HOUSE

Even the simplest magic spell takes some time and concentration to cast. So, if you're going to attack a witch, catch her off guard. Like when she first gets home and hasn't even set down her grocery bags yet—and definitely hasn't yet reactivated the wards around her property. And is being harassed by a feline-reptile crowd of supplicants.

My kitchen door burst open. A lean, muscular man sprinted inside, dove, and tackled me, landing atop me on the floor and knocking the wind out of me.

As I was going down, I realized it was Burt Umber.

My peeps, my posse, my animal family members, shot out of the kitchen and went into hiding, leaving me to my fate.

"Why have you been like a rash on my butt?" asked Umber, sitting atop me as I lay on my stomach on the kitchen floor. Drops of his sweat landed on the tile beside my face.

"You should try to keep your butt dry when you're on your

167

boat," I said, barely able to breathe and speak. "If you don't want a rash."

"You crazy freak," he said, panting. "Don't even think of doing whatever you did in my houseboat, or I'll kill you right away."

I don't believe he knew that the fact I was face-down on the floor, unable to see him, prevented me from casting my best defensive spells.

Yeah, I could use my prime elementals to conjure up a windstorm or earthquake, but that would do more to destroy my home than to save me.

But I had other, more minor, spells up my sleeve.

"You've been spying on my home, following me around, asking people about me," he said. "What's wrong with you?"

"Don't take this personally, but I believe you're a murderer?"

"*What?*"

"I believe you killed Puttle, Charles Chubb, and, possibly, Todd Oddbelly. Maybe even Billy Lee Jacobs."

"Are you out of your mind?"

"No. I'm not on any of the drugs you're peddling."

"Was that you I saw spying on my boat in Port Inferno?" he asked. "Those were boxes of oysters."

"Oysters from Colombia. Is that what you sell to Elizabeth Chubb?"

"It's time you minded your own business," he said in a low, chilling voice.

"I know you run drugs for the Colombian cartel."

"You're not making a good case for keeping you alive."

"I happen to know Felix Carrascal," I said. "We're friends. Sort of."

"Sure, you are. He's upset that a lunatic like you saw me delivering . . . oysters. And thanks to you, I have a lady cop following me around."

The spell I was casting activated. I know it wasn't much of a defensive spell. But speak to any skunk, and they'd tell you that offensive odors can be pretty effective.

"Oh, man! What did you do?" he whined. "What the heck did you have for dinner?"

"Nothing. Because a certain intruder is preventing me from making dinner."

He got off me and stood up, stepping one foot away, covering his face with the crook of his elbow.

But he also pulled out a gun with his other hand and aimed it at me. He didn't appear to intend to shoot me right away, though.

I rolled over onto my back, building my truth spell. It would be a long shot making this work, considering the situation I was in. But if I could reach my hand into my pocket and get a pinch of the powder . . .

"What are you doing?" he asked nervously. "Do you have a weapon in there?"

"No. It's potpourri. To mask this awful odor."

I withdrew my hand from my pocket and tossed the powder onto his shoes while his gun was still aimed at me.

"It's not working," he said. "It still smells in here like a skunk sprayed a port-a-potty at a rock concert."

His eyes had that manic, glassy look.

"Did you murder Jerome Puttle?" I asked in a whisper.

169

"No. Not that I hadn't fantasized about it. But someone beat me to it."

"Did you murder Charles Chubb?"

"No. I had no reason to do that. Elizabeth was free to date me."

"What about Billy Lee Jacobs and Todd Oddbelly?"

"I'm not sure if I know who they are. But no, I didn't kill them."

His responses seemed sincere. There was no struggle to control himself like I'd witnessed in Shortle. The problem was, he had just dismantled my elaborate conspiracy theory.

"Are you sure you didn't kill anybody?"

"I killed a dude twenty years ago," he said. "But that's none of your business."

"Then why—"

The hole appeared in my kitchen window a fraction of a second before the gunshot echoed outside.

Umber's knees buckled, just as a second gunshot rang out from my yard, and he dropped to the floor.

Umber lay unconscious on my kitchen floor with a wound to his head. My nurse's training kicked in.

I grabbed a dishrag and pushed it against the wound with my left hand, while my right probed his carotid artery in his neck, searching for a pulse.

There was no pulse.

I was sitting astride him, doing chest compressions in the futile hope that his heart would beat again, when Shortle walked into my kitchen from the front door.

She held a gun in her hand, pointed safely toward the floor. It reeked of having just been fired.

"Is he dead?" she asked.

"Call nine-one-one!" I shouted.

"He looks dead."

"He has no pulse, but I can't give up on him yet."

"I didn't realize you care for him so deeply."

"I'm a nurse, Shortle. You know how it is when training kicks in."

"I do."

Several minutes later, after the ambulance arrived and I'd let the paramedics take over, I remained sitting on the floor, huffing and puffing from the CPR.

When the paramedics rolled the gurney from my kitchen, I could tell by their attitude that the patient was gone.

"Did you shoot him?" I asked Shortle.

"No! Absolutely not. I followed him to your house, and I heard a gunshot. A car escaped from the scene, and I fired my weapon at it. I didn't follow procedure, but I knew the car held the shooter."

"Yeah, right," I said sarcastically. "I didn't hear a car speeding away."

I looked out the window near the bullet hole, which hadn't caused shattering because it was impact-resistant glass for hurricanes. Shortle's car sat in my driveway, and the car I'd barely noticed before was still parked across the street.

After all, its driver, Umber, was dead.

"I'm certain Carrascal ordered Umber to be killed," Shortle said. "Thanks to you, bringing attention to him from the boss."

"Don't try to make me feel guilty. Why did you tell me to stay away from Umber? Were you using him to get to Carrascal?"

"You know I can't answer that."

"He might have been shot because of you," I said.

Or maybe, you shot him yourself, I thought, but couldn't say aloud to an officer with a freshly fired gun.

So much for my plans for a relaxing evening. Detective Glasbag and a uniformed officer showed up, closely followed by the crime-scene unit. Shortle received a call, then confirmed to us the obvious, that Umber was dead on arrival at the hospital. From snippets of conversation I heard, officer-involved shootings require lots of extra paperwork.

Try getting two cats to eat when strangers are stomping around inside your house. I found Tony eating in the garage with gusto, but, of course, he complained about the racket. I explained what it was all about.

"You gotta be kidding me! Shortle shot a dude in our house?"

"I think she did. She claims an unknown shooter did it, and she shot at the shooter. But it seems suspicious to me."

"You really think it was her? Is she the angel of death who's been killing the people Matt is blamed for?"

"She was my second choice. My prime suspect, Umber, is dead now."

"Let me get this straight," Tony said, pausing his munching on an orchid leaf. "Shortle is going around executing bad guys and lowlifes just because she doesn't like them?"

"There have been cop serial killers before."

"Really?"

"Well, I read about one in Florida back in the seventies. But he was a psycho sex killer, so it's not an apples-to-apples comparison. I'm just saying it can happen."

"It seems like a big stretch."

"I know," I said. "I guess I'm desperate to get Matt out of jail. The justice system is failing him."

"Am I detecting feelings of love for Pencil Neck?"

"You know I'm fond of him. And stop calling him that."

"Be patient," he said, his mouth full of orchid. Wait, was it one of mine? "And don't do anything foolish."

AFTER EVERYONE HAD CLEARED out of my house, their trash collected, and the kitchen floor cleaned, I tried to relax with a glass of wine.

That's when I went against Tony's advice and did something foolish. I listened to my mother.

Yes, my house had resembled Grand Central Station, with all the people coming and going. Not long after law enforcement left, Ruth showed up. As usual, she simply appeared in my living room without knocking.

Sipping my wine, I watched her warily.

"You want a glass?" I asked.

"You got a beer?"

"Yeah. Hang on."

I went to the garage and got a beer from the extra fridge where I keep perishable ingredients for spells and beer for Matt.

"Evil has entered the house," Tony said.

"I know. Hopefully, she'll leave soon."

I brought the bottle to Ruth, and she opened it with her

teeth, spitting the bottle cap onto the floor. Always a classy lady.

"You're overdue in fulfilling your next task for me," she said, before taking a gulp of beer.

"I've been busy."

"You were hoping to procrastinate until your sweetie's charges were dropped so you wouldn't have to break him out. But he's still in there."

"You know this because of your magic?"

"No. Because of the internet. The jail lists all their inmates. And I got this for you."

She unfolded a piece of paper from her purse. It was covered with pencil drawings.

"One of my worshippers, a Knight Simplar, recently spent an all-inclusive vacation at the Crab County Jail. He gave me this floor plan in case you need it."

"Um, I don't think I can fulfill your assignment."

"Stop your caterwauling and listen. You're skilled enough to accomplish this with magic, and I'll show you how."

"But I'd rather get him out legitimately. If he escapes, he could be shot and killed. Even if he survives, he'll be on the run for the rest of his life. His career will be over, and he'll have to take on a false identity. Same for me. All of this just to stroke your ego?"

I feared I had enraged her, but she merely cackled and lit a cigarette.

"Please don't smoke in here."

"Yes, you're going to break him out to stroke my ego. But also, to prove to yourself how powerful you can be. And don't worry about Matt living on the lam. After you present him to me, you're going to put him back in the jail."

"What? Are you crazy? Break him out just to put him back? That will be devastating to him."

"So, which is worse? Ruining his career or putting him back in the slammer after a little excursion?"

"Well . . ."

"Think of it like him leaving jail temporarily for an outside doctor's appointment. Which is how you're going to pull it off. It's quite a clever plan, if I say so myself."

"You have a complete plan for this?"

"Yes. I knew you would need lots of handholding. This is how it will work: Matt will develop a heart condition. Atrial fibrillation, to be exact."

"Oh my. That's serious."

"We're just going to mimic it with magic. Next time he calls you, you'll send the spell over the phone to mess up his heart's rhythm temporarily. He'll go to the infirmary, where they won't have the resources to treat this. So, they'll send him to a cardiologist on the outside. Are you still with me?"

"Yeah," I replied. "How will I know where they're sending him?"

"You have a locator spell, don't you?"

I nodded.

"As he's leaving his doctor's appointment, that's when you make the switch."

"The switch?"

"Let me finish. He'll be under guard, of course, so you'll need an invisibility spell."

"I don't have one."

"Then you'd better learn one, quickly."

I had been wanting to create one, so I didn't complain.

"So, you'll go to the doctor's office, invisible. Before they put the cuffs and shackles on Matt and put him in the jail's van, you'll make him invisible and replace him with his doppelgänger."

"Wait, what?"

"His body double. An identical Matt. You'll need black magic to do that. The perfect introduction to all this glorious power you've been missing."

"I don't know . . ."

"Stop being a baby. After you make the substitution, you'll bring the real Matt to me while the doppelgänger is taken to the jail. It's that easy."

"You think the guards will really be fooled?"

"Yes. The doppelgänger will be very convincing."

"So, why does the real Matt need to return to jail? Let's just leave the doppelgänger there."

"Because his double has an expiration date. It will fade away in twenty-four hours or so. Plus, doppelgängers aren't very intelligent. They wouldn't be able to deal with lawyers and court proceedings."

"Okay. How do I return Matt to jail?"

"That's the hard part. You'll need this floor plan to get Matt into the facility, and to his cell, while you're both invisible. He'll replace the doppelgänger, and you'll get the heck out of Dodge."

"This is an awful lot of work to stroke your ego," I said.

"It's meant to stroke yours, too. Pull this off successfully, and you'll see what I mean about your potential. But first, you have two powerful spells to learn."

CHAPTER 18
INVISIBLE

The next day, right after the window guy gave me an estimate for replacing the bullet-damaged pane, I convened my Brain Trust. This consortium of wise, magical minds included yours truly, the ghost of a seventeenth-century wizard, and a talking iguana. Not since the moon landing have such great minds worked together to solve a critical challenge.

Namely, how to make Missy invisible.

"You wish to create this spell in order to get inside a prison?" Don Mateo asked. "Perchance, getting arrested would be an easier way to do so."

"You weren't listening closely when I explained the plan," I said. "Aside from needing it for this mission, I've wanted an invisibility spell ever since I began trying to solve mysteries."

"So, you can spy on your suspects?"

"Exactly."

"This spell better not have any flaws," Tony said. "It

wouldn't be good if a pretty chick like you suddenly appeared in the men's wing of the jail."

"Egads! That would be horrible!" Don Mateo exclaimed.

"Get your so-called brilliant minds out of the gutter and help me devise this spell. We need to find a basic framework, and I can build the spell on top of that."

"What do you mean by framework?" Tony asked.

"She means," Don Mateo explained, "a matter-displacement spell, elemental-energy spell, organic-material spell—classifications like that."

"I'm not a dead wizard or a live witch, but based on my many years as a familiar, I'd say build it on the chassis of a sensory-disorder spell," Tony suggested. "In other words, the magic doesn't alter *you*. It affects the vision of everyone else, so they can see everything except you."

"Very clever, reptile," said Don Mateo. "But what if someone is observing her from afar, beyond the spell's reach? I would say a magical field that deflects rays of light from reaching you would work."

"Wouldn't you then see a dark shadow of a witch?"

"Keep the ideas coming, guys," I said. "Remember, there are no bad ideas."

"Yeah, there are," Tony said. "Don Mateo is dead because of a bad idea."

"Summoning the demon seemed like it would be an amusing party trick," the wizard said.

"It was amusing for the demon."

"Listen guys," I said. "I think I'll sort of combine your ideas."

"You sound like someone in corporate America," Tony quipped.

"Let me finish. The spell will alter the light rays after they hit me, when they bounce off. Any eyes, near or far, will see the altered rays, which will reveal everything in the scene except for me."

"Brilliant!" Don Mateo said.

"Having lived through the centuries of discovery in physics since my friend Don Mateo left the earthly realm," Tony said, "I dunno. I expect a bald guy in a lab coat to pop in here and say it can't work."

"That's the beauty of magic," I said. "It works in a world defined by the rules of science, but it breaks a lot of those rules. Which is a victory for people like me who only got Bs in physics."

"Rules are meant to be broken," Don Mateo said. "An expression that was common even back in my day."

"Very well, then! If we combine your two ideas, I think we should use an elemental-energy spell structure. Based on the element of fire, since we're talking about light."

"You two are the magicians," Tony said. "How do we do that?"

"We find an existing spell that was built upon the same structure," Don Mateo said. "Magic is like art. We borrow and steal as much as we invent." He chuckled. "I remember an old spell I used when I was a witch, in training to become a wizard. It was mainly for our amusement."

"This better not be a demon-summoning spell," Tony said.

"No, no. I called it the Lamp Spell. At night, or in a dark

room, it gathered the tiniest bits of ambient light in the area, condensed them into a single orb, and amplified it." He laughed. "If your amigo was in a dark closet using a chamber pot, he'd suddenly be exposed to the light of a hundred suns!"

He continued to laugh like this was the best joke in the world.

"I'm glad we didn't hang out together back then," Tony said. "We had different ideas of humor."

"You were a dog back then, Tony. A lapdog. A Cavalier King Charles Spaniel. You didn't have a sense of humor."

"I was the familiar to a witch who was powerful and successful and didn't end up devoured by a demon."

"Kids, let's work together," I said. "You're my Brain Trust. You've both been around for centuries. Please don't act like six-year-olds."

"Whatever you say, madam," Don Mateo said with a sigh. Or a sound like a sigh, since ghosts don't expel air. "I'll walk you through casting my lamp spell. You can study its construction, and we can see if it's suitable to be the basic building blocks of your invisibility spell."

Don Mateo and I worked through it until late at night, with Tony throwing in some suggestions. I was uncool enough to use a whiteboard to take notes and make schematic sketches of the spell's structure, as if it were a science project and not arcane magic. Around 2:00 a.m., I broke up the Brain Trust session because I needed to sleep.

The following day was my day off from the botanica, so we spent it brainstorming how to cast the spell, section by section, while I composed the words of the incantation.

Later, I tested the various sections to see if they worked. I felt more like a software coder than a witch, but I didn't have the luxury of being able to tinker with this spell for years. It had to be foolproof as soon as possible.

Close to midnight, I assembled the sections of the spell and cast it in its entirety. I didn't use a magic circle, because that would be impractical when it came time to use it for Matt's escape. However, holding the Red Dragon talisman gave me the extra power I needed.

I cast the spell in my bedroom with all the lights turned on, sending their illumination at me from different directions. The spell was supposed to block the light waves bouncing off me that someone would use to see me.

When I was finished, I felt depleted from the huge amount of energy I had pumped into the spell. But nothing else about me felt different.

Until I looked into the mirror above my dresser.

I simply wasn't there. The mirror reflected the room behind me, but without me. I waved my hands, and nothing registered.

"Tony! Don Mateo! I think I've got it! Come here and see for yourselves."

Tony padded into the room and glanced in my direction, confusion on his lizard face.

Seconds later, Don Mateo materialized. He looked me up and down, frowning.

"You guys are both looking at me, even though I haven't spoken to give away where I am. Are you just assuming I'd be in front of the mirror?"

"Ahem, uh, no, m'lady," said Don Mateo.

"I've got good news and bad news," Tony said.

"Go ahead. Tell me."

"You've done a remarkable job of attaining invisibility," Don Mateo said. "From the waist up."

"What?"

"We can see your legs and butt," Tony added. "You look like half a department store mannequin."

I looked down. They were absolutely correct.

"Oh my. I don't know what I did wrong. There could be a flaw in the incantation," I said, pacing back and forth across the room, picturing the spell's structure in my mind.

"Will you stand still? Your two legs walking around by themselves are freaking me out," Tony said.

"Yeah, I think it's the incantation. I used a Latin word that has more than one meaning."

"You must be precise," Don Mateo advised. "Release the spell, then cast it again, replacing the Latin word with one in modern English that cannot be misinterpreted."

I released the spell, and my image reappeared in the mirror. Though I worried my internal energies were too depleted, I tried casting the spell again, using the revised incantation.

"Bravo!" Don Mateo exclaimed. "Success at last!"

There was no one in the mirror. And looking down, I saw nothing. I went into the bathroom where I have a full-length mirror, and there was no one in it.

I picked up a hairbrush, which appeared to float on its own. I splashed water from the sink onto my face. The water droplets that clung to my skin seemed to hang in the air before fading away as they evaporated or were absorbed into my skin.

This sucker worked.

I applied lipstick, the light plum shade I usually wear when I wear any at all.

A lip-shaped entity hung in the air, as if I had kissed the mirror and left a lipstick impression on it.

I returned to my bedroom and put on a baseball cap. When I looked in the mirror, I saw a floating baseball cap and lip-shaped lipstick.

"You're freaking me out," Tony said.

"I know."

I absorbed the lesson. At the moment I cast the invisibility spell, all of me—and everything on me, such as my clothing—became invisible.

Yet everything I put on afterward was not invisible. I must not forget this, or I might get caught when using the spell.

"How long do you think the spell will last?" I asked Don Mateo.

"There is only one way to find out, m'lady."

So, I glanced at my watch and went about doing some housework to kill time. If Tony was freaked out, you should have seen how Brenda and Bubba behaved. Smelling me, but not seeing me, and watching my broom operate on its own, sent the two cats into hiding, possibly forever.

About ninety minutes after casting the spell, parts of me began to reappear. A flash of my leg here, a blurred glimpse of my moving hand there. In my foyer mirror, I watched myself come into being again. It was like the old-fashioned method of making photographic prints in a darkroom, the chemicals bringing the image to life.

"Okay," I said to any of my Brain Trust still listening. "Next,

I must learn the doppelgänger spell. I'm really dreading trying my hand at black magic."

My phone rang. It was the county jail's phone service I was paying for. I had also sent money to his commissary account, so he could buy snacks and incidentals. All of this was blatantly overpriced, and yet another reason for you or your loved ones to avoid going to jail.

For Matt, it hadn't been possible to avoid, even though he was innocent.

After a few minutes of small talk, in which he lamented the nightmare he was experiencing, and I offered my condolences, he asked me if I had any new developments.

"Umber is dead," I said.

"You've got to be kidding."

"I wish I was." I gave a short explanation of what had happened but couldn't say too much because the call was probably being recorded.

"Do you have any new leads for my defense?"

"I'll communicate that through Paul Leclerc. He'll fill you in when he visits you next."

Despite my truth spell seeming to have exonerated Umber, part of me still hoped he was responsible for the murders. The spell wasn't perfect, after all. And the fact that he was now dead wouldn't change his culpability.

If not him, I would blame Carrascal for eliminating people he believed witnessed drug-smuggling activity, though that didn't explain Chubb's death. If not Carrascal, my pick would be Shortle. Or there could have been more than one murderer.

My mind, though, was focused on the risky attempt to

bring Matt to Ruth. Of course, I couldn't say anything to Matt about it.

"How's your heart?" I asked. "Still feeling arrhythmias? You should get that looked at soon by a specialist."

Matt was silent. He was smart enough to assume I was using coded language, even though I was being very literal.

"Call me in two days," I said. "It's very important. I miss you."

We traded non-committal endearments before hanging up.

In two days, I should be ready to cast the spell to alter his heart's rhythm. And as the reality of what I was about to do struck me, I became overwhelmed with guilt.

The spell for his heart would be harmless, but it would scare the heck out of him. And then, he would go through the danger of my abducting him during his doctor's visit.

Worst of all, after presenting Matt to Ruth, I would need to return him to jail.

What was wrong with me? How could I be so selfish and cruel? Matt hadn't agreed to go through all this trauma just so I could join Ruth's coven and spy on her.

I believed bringing Ruth down would benefit everyone in the community, including Matt, and not just the werewolves, brainwashed witches, and me.

Remember, Ruth promised to kill me if I didn't join her coven, and she wouldn't allow me to join without passing her stupid tests.

Matt would put his life at risk to save mine. I knew he would. But being manipulated like this seemed like too much of a price for him to pay.

I should say no to the deal.

As if someone was reading my thoughts, the doorbell rang. I actually hoped it was Mrs. Lupis and Mr. Lopez, so I could cry on their shoulders. Metaphorically, of course. I doubted they would let me touch them.

Alas, no. It was the last person I wanted to see during my dark moment of the soul.

Fred Furman.

CHAPTER 19
DOPPELGÄNGER

"Sorry to stop by without an invitation," Furman said, looking jaundiced in the yellow lighting of my front porch.

In his human form, he was just a short, pudgy old guy with thick, luxurious white hair. There was nothing about him that implied he was a werewolf, nor that he was the informal alpha of the local merchant wolves.

Recently, the local merchants had all been dominated, and extorted, by a city councilman. But after the councilman was defeated, Furman enjoyed a brief reign as alpha again. Until my mother tried to take over the town, forcing the werewolf merchants to pay protection money like the councilman had.

"If you're here to check on my progress with Ruth, I haven't joined the coven yet," I told him. "She's assigning me ridiculous tasks to prove that I'm worthy and loyal."

Of course, I could never tell Furman what the tasks were.

IN SPRITE OF HERSELF

"She's your mother, right? Why do you need to prove anything?"

"As I told you, she is my biological mother, and I knew nothing about her until a few years ago. In fact, you could say we've been antagonists ever since. I don't blame her for not trusting me, because I don't trust her, either."

Furman pawed at his ear, which was being harassed by a gnat.

"Please come in," I said, ushering him into the living room. "Can I get you something to drink?"

"You wouldn't happen to have any Scotch, would you?"

"I do, in fact."

"Straight up, please."

I went into the kitchen to get the bottle of single malt that Angela had given me, even though I could barely tolerate the stuff.

I served him a glass of the whisky, while I had wine. He looked at me nervously as he sipped.

"Just so you know, I'm working on Ruth's second task," I said. "It's very complex and dangerous. I hope, if I complete it, that I'll be done with proving myself."

"Good to hear. She's really turning the screws on the Downtown Merchants Association. Those of us who are were-wolves, that is. She's demanding more money from us each month and roughing up anyone who misses a payment."

"Roughing up how?"

"Annie's Fine Interiors got trashed the other night. We think her goons, the Knights Simplar, did it."

I nodded. "I'm not surprised."

"And Joe the hairstylist. She turned him into a frog."

"He always kind of reminded me of a frog."

"It's not funny," Furman snapped. "I'm serious. He's a frog now. I've had to step in to hire a replacement for him so he doesn't go out of business, and I loaned him money for his missed protection payment. We're still waiting for Ruth to turn him back."

"I'm sorry."

"Look, you have to go through with whatever it takes to get inside her coven."

"I told you I am. But once I'm inside, what are you planning to do? I'll give you any information I learn, but how, exactly, are you planning to take her down and run her out of town? Her magic is unbelievably powerful."

"I know. We need you to be more than a spy. You're going to learn her magic and discover her weaknesses so you can use them against her."

"Wait a minute—"

"No, you knew that was part of the deal if you join her coven. Learning black magic."

I looked away. "Yeah. A little of it."

To be honest, the doppelgänger spell she was going to teach me didn't sound like a "little" spell.

"We werewolves are fearsome fighters, but we can't defeat black magic. We need you to do it. She's going to kill some of us if we don't act soon."

"That sounds a little extreme. Why would she kill the geese that lay the golden eggs? She has a lucrative arrangement here."

"Don't you ever wonder why she came to Jellyfish Beach?"

"I assumed it had something to do with me, but maybe I'm overly sentimental."

"She was driven out of North Florida by the magic guilds after she killed some people. That's why she wants to build a giant coven—to fight back against anyone trying to give her accountability. She's evil. Sorry, no offense."

"None taken. I know she's evil."

And I knew she was capable of killing. I just didn't think she would complicate her life by doing so. I guess I was wrong.

"I stopped by tonight to fortify you, like this Scotch is fortifying me." Furman took a deep sip. "We can't afford to have you go wobbly on us."

"Me? Wobbly? I might be flaky, but not wobbly."

He chuckled. "Anyone could get wobbly when facing an evil black-magic sorceress and the demons she consorts with. But you're our only hope, Missy. And by 'our,' I mean all of us living in Jellyfish Beach."

Go ahead, put the weight of the world on my shoulders, I thought. Like that's not going to make me go wobbly.

"Worry not, Fred. I won't let you down."

I meant what I said. Although I feared by doing this, I would let Matt down.

THEY WERE WAITING FOR ME.

The door to Ruth's apartment opened to reveal at least thirty acolytes bathed in candlelight, their faces turned to me expectantly.

The large living-dining room had been cleared of furniture,

and the coven members sat on the floor around its perimeter. About a dozen of them were the Knights Simplar, wearing their ceremonial tunics. The rest were witches, some men, but mostly women, of a wide range of ages.

Many of the witches were familiar to me as customers of The Jellyfish Beach Mystical Mart & Botanica. The others got their supplies elsewhere or on the internet. Only a handful of the witches lived in Jellyfish Beach proper; the rest were from surrounding towns.

In the center of the room was a large circle around an inverted pentagram. They were painted red. I hoped it was paint and not blood. Black candles burned at the five points of the pentagram, adding to the dancing light of the candles in wall sconces and on candelabras around the room.

An older woman I'd seen here before led the acolytes in a low chant. The language was foreign and strange. It was an ugly, guttural tongue that seemed both ancient and evil.

Even though all eyes were on me, no one spoke to me. I stood outside the circle, unsure of what to do.

Then came the familiar cackle. Ruth emerged from a hallway leading to the bedrooms. She wore black robes with an inverted pentagram in silver hanging from a necklace.

"All hail Saint Ruthless," the room said in unison as everyone prostrated themselves to their leader.

"Ready to learn something really cool?" she asked me.

I shrugged.

The leotard man came from the kitchen, carrying a small black cauldron that emitted a foul, sulfuric odor. He placed it in the center of the magic circle, bowed to it, then left. He returned with a black cloak that he draped over me.

"Join me in the circle," Ruth said to me as she stepped between acolytes and entered the circle.

She kneeled, facing me, the cauldron between us, and gestured for me to do the same.

"We assemble here humbly to beg the assistance of the legions of demons who rule the darkness, and the ancient gods who ruled the universe before the dawn of time," Ruth intoned in a low voice. "I offer you my daughter to be your vessel as you lend her your powers."

She gave me a piercing stare.

"Do you accept the dark lords and honor them?"

"Yes," I replied, though I spoke without conviction.

"I call upon Asmodeus, the king of demons, to come before us. Asmodeus, I summon thee!"

She reached into a pocket of her robe and tossed a handful of something into the cauldron. A geyser of flame shot upward, almost to the ceiling, drawing awed murmurs from the crowd.

"Asmodeus, reveal thyself!"

The flame in the cauldron died and a wind suddenly swept through the room, blowing out all the candles and leaving us in total darkness.

"What is your request?" asked a raspy, slimy, reptilian voice that came from somewhere above the magic circle.

"I beg of you to endow my daughter, Missy Mindle, with the power to duplicate living creatures, to create doppelgängers that will obey her every command. Give me your left hand, Missy."

I reached over the cauldron, which had begun to glow faintly, providing the only light in the room. Ruth took my hand, spreading it open, palm up.

A sharp, searing pain went across my palm—the incision from a knife blade.

"Her blood will bind you to her, Asmodeus, when she requests you to create a doppelgänger of whichever creature she specifies. Now, you will create the duplicate of the person I am picturing in my mind."

An icy wind rustled through the room again, making me shiver. Something immaterial invaded me and tugged at my soul.

We all sat in silence for what seemed like an eternity. Until the footsteps sounded in the hall leading from the bedrooms.

Someone walked into the room. With the only light coming from the glowing cauldron, I could only make out a silhouette standing there outside of the circle. I believed it was female.

Suddenly, all the candles burned again. In the light, the person who had come into the room was revealed. I gasped.

It was me.

A perfect twin of forty-something me stood there, the same long straight hair and green eyes, the same black cloak. She looked at me expectantly, awaiting my commands.

"What do you think?" Ruth asked. "Pretty good, huh?"

"I can't believe it," I whispered.

She cackled with amusement. "The power of black magic."

Briefly, I considered ordering my doppelgänger to attack Ruth. Next, I thought about ordering her to distract the crowd so I could slip out of the apartment and my twin would join the coven instead of me.

But I couldn't stand the thought of another me existing, obeying all the evil commands of Ruth.

"Say goodbye to your better half," Ruth said, as if she'd read my mind. "She was here for demonstration purposes only. When I say, 'Depart, doppelgänger,' clap your hands three times."

I nodded.

"Depart, doppelgänger," she commanded.

I clapped, making the wound in my palm sting.

The other Missy was gone.

"See how easy that was?" Ruth asked. "When it's time to create the doppelgänger of your friend, cut your left palm again with this knife." She handed me an ancient dagger with a bone handle. "And command Asmodeus to create him. And when you need the duplicate no longer, order him to leave and clap your hands, making sure you reopen the wound and draw blood."

"That's it? No powders or potions? No gathering of energies? No incantation?"

"Asmodeus will do the heavy lifting for as long as I bind him to you. All you need to do is supply the blood."

"Wow."

"Isn't it a rush to wield all that power?"

"It's kind of scary," I said. "I don't trust demons. My biological father was killed by one that you summoned."

"That was all just a big misunderstanding."

"A fatal one."

"Stop being so negative. Get out there and do something heroic. Free your friend from jail and bring him to me. And then you can join our family."

Family. As if these brainwashed fools sitting on the floor were anything other than cult members.

THE CALL from the jail came the next evening. The spell I created, with my white magic, traveled across the electronic connection between Matt and me. It temporarily affected the heart's electrical system that controls heartbeats—the organ's pumping of blood in and out of its chambers. I had created the spell years ago to heal arrhythmia, but in Matt's healthy heart, it produced the opposite effect, creating the condition.

"I feel kind of weird," Matt said in a breathy voice.

"You need to go to the jail infirmary. They'll do their best, but you'll probably need to see a specialist, an electrophysiologist. Let me know when you'll do that."

The mission to free Matt had begun.

And I felt rotten to my core.

Of course, that's when my doorbell rang. It always rings just when I'm on the verge of losing my mind.

Mrs. Lupis and Mr. Lopez stood on my front porch.

"We have an urgent problem," they said together.

I was so tempted to slam the door in their faces.

CHAPTER 20
SPRITE SPAT

"What," I asked with irritation of my Society handlers, "is the big problem?"

"Sprites," replied Mr. Lopez.

"Specifically, the new crested mouth sprite in our territory," Mrs. Lupis added. "She's been muscling in on the neighboring territories claimed by other sprites."

"Why would she do that?"

"She claims we don't have enough kids losing teeth here. She's not getting enough psychic energy from her nightly tooth-fairy visits."

"Why is this our concern?" I asked, perhaps naively.

"We'll let the clan chieftain explain."

A buzzing too loud for such small, gossamer wings filled my ears as the eighteen-inch-tall crested mouth sprite flew through the open door into my foyer. She looked like Rachel did in her natural form, except the crest atop the chieftain's head was covered in golden glitter.

"Missy Mindle, meet the Chieftain Lady Boldfly," Mr. Lopez announced.

In the blink of my eye, she shifted into a human form. Unlike Rachel, she had a more sophisticated appearance. True, her face was crone-like, and she had more than her share of tattoos. But she was, in a word, genteel.

"You are the local agent of the Friends of Cryptids Society?" she asked me.

"Yes. Well, there are others, like Angela."

"Per the recent treaty between my clan and your organization, you may study our clan members if you provide policing services for us."

"Policing?"

"We are fragile and few," Chieftain Lady Boldfly said. "That is why it took so long for your Society to find us. It also means we are vulnerable to attack from faeries, pixies, and our own species."

"You want us to be your muscle? Your soldiers?"

"Precisely. I have contacted Rachel and ordered her to be less overbearing and more respectful to the others in our clan. Unfortunately, politeness goes against her nature."

I turned to Mrs. Lupis and Mr. Lopez. "Are you guys going to stand up for me? I can't make sure the tooth fairy doesn't misbehave. We would need to hire an entire team to track Rachel's every move to catch her straying onto someone else's territory."

"The treaty we signed does not mandate constant surveillance of your clan members," Mr. Lopez said.

"That's not what I am requesting," Chieftain Lady Boldfly

said. "I only wish for you to respond when Rachel commits an offense. Here, I shall make it easy for you."

She handed me a fossilized tooth, smooth and blackened with age. It appeared to be a molar, but from what creature?

"That's a tooth from an immature *Homo erectus*, an ancestor of modern humans. As you can see, tooth fairies have been at this for literally a million years."

"What do I do with it?" I asked.

"It has a magical connection to the psychic energy our sprites collect from baby teeth. It will alert you if a conflict between sprites creates a disturbance in the energy field, and it should help you find where it's happening."

"Pretty cool."

"Your request is reasonable," Mrs. Lupis said. "We're happy to oblige."

"I expect you to return the tooth after this matter has been resolved," said the sprite before she shifted back to her true form and flew out my door.

"Angela can respond to misbehaving sprites," I said. "That's her job as an enforcer."

"Yes, but you need to be her eyes and ears," Mrs. Lupis said.

"This is not a good time for me. As you know, Matt is in jail, and I'm trying to exonerate him. Meanwhile, I have some heavy obligations with my evil sorceress mother."

The two looked at me without a trace of sympathy.

"And a full-time job at the botanica," I added.

"You knew the terms of the contract when you received our grant," said Mrs. Lupis.

"Yeah, to help you discover and catalog monsters—cryptids

and unusual supernatural creatures—that Luisa and I come across while running the botanica."

My handlers shook their heads.

Mrs. Lupis suddenly produced a sheaf of papers. From where, I didn't know.

"As you see here in Section Five, Subsection Three, it states, 'You will monitor the existence of unusual creatures in all of Jellyfish Beach and its adjacent neighborhoods.'"

"Let me see that." I grabbed the contract from her. The wording didn't sound familiar, but maybe I hadn't read the contract closely enough during the exciting days when we signed it.

"Did you read your contract close—"

"I did!" I snapped.

"No need to get snippy."

"The Society invested a lot of money in the botanica," I said. "My priority should be to make sure the business is profitable."

"That's for sure," Mr. Lopez said.

"You were not completely forthcoming with us when you signed this contract," said Mrs. Lupis.

"What do you mean?" I was a bit nervous after her comment. Since I wasn't sure what kinds of creatures my handlers actually were, I didn't want to push the wrong buttons.

"You're complaining about your obligations regarding your evil sorceress mother. You never mentioned her when you sealed the deal with us. Why should we be penalized for all the time you say you need to spend on her?"

"And an evil sorceress could lead you astray from our mission," said Mr. Lopez.

"It wasn't an issue back then. It has escalated with her threatening to kill me if I don't join her coven."

"You realize there's a non-compete clause in the contract, right?" Mrs. Lupis asked.

"My mother is personally acquainted with several demons. Don't you guys want information on them?"

"Technically, demons aren't cryptids."

"But they are supernatural beings we would love to study," Mr. Lopez interjected.

His partner glared at him. I got the vibe that they might be more than just work partners.

"When you feel overwhelmed, you need to prioritize," Mrs. Lupis said with an obviously fake smile. "Yes, your chief priority is the botanica. But it is followed closely by monitoring and managing monsters in our area. Getting friends out of jail and appeasing your mother are way down the list."

I nodded. When they saw the frown on my face, my handlers seemed to realize they'd gone as far as they could.

"Have a lovely evening," Mr. Lopez said as they hurried out of my foyer.

I WAS ASLEEP, having gone to bed early for the first time in weeks. I'd been determined to catch up on all the sleep lost from amateur sleuthing and vampire home-health visits. Remind me to stop accepting vampire appointment requests.

A weird vibrating sound woke me up. It wasn't coming

from my phone, which was on the nightstand beside me. The rattling came from the top of my dresser.

I switched on my bedside light and discovered the source of the noise. The fossilized molar the sprite chieftain had lent me was dancing all over the dresser like an enraged bumble bee.

Obviously, there was a disturbance in the psychic energy field the sprites depended upon. I assumed Rachel was most likely the troublemaker causing the disturbance.

I got out of bed and went to the dresser, watching the tooth bounce around. What was I supposed to do now? How was I supposed to find out where the trouble was occurring? Sure, I have magic in my blood, but I can't just snap my fingers and expect answers.

There was nothing else to do but hold the tooth and see if I could read what it was trying to tell me. Catching it wasn't easy. But with both hands, I captured it mid-leap.

And yelped as it burned my hand. How did this thing get so hot? The psychic energy was much stronger than I had expected. It was so strong that as I forced myself to hang on to the hot tooth, I—

Flew above a suburban neighborhood in the night sky. Muscles pulsed in my back as my insect-like wings kept me aloft. I looked down at the typical Florida mixture of shingle, stucco, and metals roofs arrayed along empty streets. This was a different town—not Jellyfish Beach.

I saw them below me: two crested mouth sprites fighting in mid-air. They fought the way mockingbirds battle crows that encroach on their nests, chasing and dive-bombing each other, making very little physical contact.

Without consciously doing so, I dropped to their altitude, just above the roof of a home.

"Hey, stop it!" I shouted.

They ignored me. It occurred to me that I wasn't here physically, only mentally. I wouldn't be able to break up this fight without coming here in person. So, like I did when using my locator spell, I noted the number of the house they were above and the street sign.

Then, somehow, I forced myself out of this hallucination, like pulling myself out of a dream. Releasing my grip on the tooth, I let it fall from my hand onto the dresser. As soon as my orientation returned, I threw on some clothes and headed for my car.

Wait. The tooth obviously had talismanic powers, so I'd better bring it with me. With it safely in my pocket, I hopped in my car and headed for the neighboring town I'd visited while under the tooth's spell.

To a normal observer, the sprites would appear to be fighting birds. The lights of the house below them were off, and all the neighboring homes were dark, as well. Hopefully, no humans were observing this.

After parking my car along the curb, I walked over to the edge of the home's lawn. Silhouetted by the stars, the two sprites continued their battle above me.

"Hey!" I called in a loud whisper, waving my arms to get the sprites' attention. "Knock it off."

I ducked as one of the lightning-fast creatures after the other sped right past my head.

"Stop it, you two! We need to talk."

And suddenly, they were hovering in front of me at eye level, both sprites in their natural forms.

"This is *my* territory," said the sprite I hadn't met before. "And that was *my* tooth in the house."

"Nonsense," said Rachel. "You were late. The child was fast asleep, and her father was about to come into her bedroom and take the tooth. Someone needed to harvest the energy from the tooth before it was disposed of."

"I got here at the same time you did. It was *my* tooth you harvested."

"It sounds like you're correct," I said to the aggrieved sprite. "What is your name?"

"I am Luna. Who are you? You smell like a witch."

"You were snooping around my territory, too," said Rachel to me. "What gives you the right to get into our business?"

"The Chieftain Lady Boldfly deputized me to maintain order," I said. "And she gave me this." I pulled the fossilized tooth from my pocket.

The sprites gasped and darted away from me. Soon, they flew back to me again warily and hovered at a greater distance from me than before.

"Your chieftain told me that you, Rachel, are causing problems. Encroaching on others' territories, just like tonight."

"There aren't enough discarded baby teeth in my territory to sustain me," she said with self-pity.

"Nonsense," Luna said. "You seem to think you have the right to do whatever you want. You told me before the witch arrived that I have more teeth than I can handle, so you're going to harvest as many as you want."

"I deserve more."

"Says who?"

"Rachel, didn't we discuss this before?" I asked. "You were being very judgmental of the humans you visited, and you promised to resist your negative inclinations."

"What does that have to do with harvesting teeth I deserve?"

"It's the arrogance of believing you know what's best and what's right. The rules say you stick to your territory. You don't get to decide that the rules don't apply to you."

Rachel landed on the grass in front of me, pouting. "It's not fair."

"You're the one who's not being fair."

"You heard the witch," taunted Luna. "Go back to your territory. It's what the chieftain wants."

Rachel muttered something in an unfamiliar language that sounded like curses before she took flight and disappeared into the night.

"Thank you," Luna said to me.

"What do you mean, I smell like a witch? What does a witch smell like? Dried herbs? Body odor?"

"Like a human with magic, of course. Excuse me, I have two more children with teeth under their pillows to visit."

After she flew away, I returned to my car. And sniffed myself out of paranoia.

Little did I know that soon I would smell like fear.

CHAPTER 21
THE GREAT ESCAPE

"I feel kinda lousy," Matt said over the phone. "My heartbeat is irregular. It's like a jazz drummer is inside my chest."

I was the worst person in the world to have done this.

"I hope you feel better soon," I said, guilt-ridden.

"They finally agreed to take me to a specialist."

"When?"

"Tomorrow."

"Good," I said. "Let me know what the doctor says."

The countdown clock was now ticking. I couldn't ask Matt any specifics about his appointment, because the call was probably being recorded, and he might not know the specifics. So, it would be up to me to find him at the doctor's office at the right time.

The only way I knew to do that was to use my locator spell and monitor his location in real time. Early in the morning of the day of his appointment, I went to his bungalow to choose a prized possession of his to use for the spell.

Yes, we have keys to each other's place. Don't rush to any conclusions. We're good friends, after all. More than friends, I guess. I pushed that from my mind as I went about callously using him to get at my mother.

He had emotional attachments to his laptop and fishing rods, but also feelings of frustration. I selected the paddle he used for paddleboarding, which he claimed relaxed him more than anything else. I could sense the positive energy on the paddle. The only negative about the sport was that it had put him near the scene of Puttle's murder. But I digress.

I brought the paddle home and placed it beside me inside the magic circle drawn on my kitchen floor. Halfway through the spell-casting process, I gripped the paddle and drew from it Matt's psychic energy. My magic converted it into a glowing orb that floated in front of my face.

I connected my senses to the orb so that I was now looking at my face from the orb's point of view.

"Go find the soul to which you belong," I commanded.

The orb sped off, the energy that created it seeking to reunite with its source: Matt.

It was like watching a drone with a camera. The orb flew over Jellyfish Beach, heading northwest toward the county jail. It passed over the barbed-wire-topped wall and descended upon the fortress-like complex. Slipping through a narrow window, it traveled to the cell where Matt slept on the top bunk.

An alteration to my spell prevented the orb from being

absorbed into Matt, as would normally happen, which would have shut off my visual and audio connection. I needed the orb to follow Matt to the doctor's office. It hovered above him, invisible to humans.

All I could do now was sit here in my trance and watch and wait for Matt to be taken there. I stared at his sleeping face with its look of childlike innocence, as if he were dreaming about life far away from this jail. Though my senses of sight and hearing were with the orb, I felt a tear running down my cheek.

I won't bore you with the details of jail routine after he woke up, but before he was allowed to go to the mess hall, two guards showed up at his cell. They handcuffed him and put his feet in shackles, then took him down to an underground parking garage where they put him into a van with heavy wire mesh over the windows.

The orb stayed with him the entire time. Which meant that I was always with him, too, unbeknownst to Matt. He looked nervous, even though he was merely going to a doctor's appointment. Then again, most of us aren't dragged shackled to our appointments under armed guard.

From the orb's vantage point inside the van, I couldn't see through the mesh-covered windows where we were going. But after it stopped, and Matt was led from the vehicle, I realized we were outside the loading dock of a medical building of some sort. A glimpse of the main hospital in the distance told me that this was the nearby outpatient facility.

I knew exactly where we were. In fact, I used to work in that hospital.

It was showtime. I released the spell and stood up, stiff and sore from my time sitting in the magic circle, and hurried to my car. Driving to the medical campus, I steeled myself for all the spell casting I had to pull off to make this mission a success.

When I reached the outpatient facility, I drove around to the rear. The prison van was still parked in the loading dock. It was a secure place for transferring a prisoner, because someone like me trying to free the prisoner could approach it from only one direction.

My watch said it was 8:30 a.m. Matt had arrived thirty minutes before. I didn't know how much longer he'd be in the office. It depended on how many diagnostic tests had been ordered. I decided to play it safe and become invisible now.

I parked my car out of view of the guards and remained in it while I cast the spell. I checked the mirror and all my extremities to make sure I was truly invisible. Then, I strolled toward the loading dock.

Walking as quietly as I could, I passed the van and climbed the short stairway to the dock platform. The two guards were right in front of me. One leaned against the wall of the building and smoked a cigarette. The other stood nearby, staring at his phone.

My heart was pounding so intensely I feared the guards would hear it. Could they see me? I got closer to them, in their peripheral vision, but they didn't look at me. Tiptoeing past them, I stationed myself between them and the double doors.

Still, they didn't look in my direction. I glanced around to make sure I wasn't leaving a shadow. Nope. So, I just stood there, hoping they wouldn't smell my fear. The one guard's cigarette smoke made that unlikely.

I tried to relax so I could go into a meditative state and

gather my internal energies along with those of the elements. I also began summoning Asmodeus.

It was critical that I get the timing right. The demon had to create Matt's doppelgänger during the short walk from the doorway to the van. And I had to make the real Matt invisible simultaneously.

The brief moment when there would be two Matts, creating confusion before the real Matt went invisible, would be my only chance to get him out of the guards' literal grasp.

"The nurse just texted," said the guard, who had been glued to his phone. "Time to get him."

They walked past without noticing me and entered the building. My heart pounded even faster.

The wait for them to exit the building was unbearable. My energies were gathered and concentrated, adding to the tension and making my ears buzz. Asmodeus was waiting in the wings, temporarily bound to me by Ruth's black magic. Having a demon nearby—especially one with human, bull, and ram heads—was never good for the nerves.

But then came the sounds of a chain clinking, and the metal doors popped open with an ominous boom.

Matt exited, flanked by the guards, each holding an arm. I involuntarily smiled when I saw him before realizing he couldn't see me.

I sliced my left palm with the ceremonial dagger near the previous wound which was only barely healed. The sensation of warm blood flowing came just before the pain hit.

"Asmodeus, I command you to make a doppelgänger of him." I pointed to Matt as he approached me.

The smell of sulfur permeated the air as a wave of evil magic swept through, making all my hairs stand on end.

Matt became blurry. It was as though I was seeing him through glasses with the wrong lenses; a second Matt was super-imposed over the first, not quite aligned. Then the two Matts separated and walked side by side, each identical down to the shackles.

Quickly, I cast the invisibility spell on the real Matt, the one whose arms were still gripped by the guards. The energy poured from me, and he disappeared.

The guards stopped, confusion on their faces. Their hands held the arms of someone who wasn't there.

"Come here," I said to the doppelgänger.

It obeyed me, walking away from the guards. They were flummoxed by the sensation of holding the arms of someone well out of their reach who was moving farther away.

"Get him!" the smoker guard shouted.

They released the invisible Matt and caught up to the doppelgänger, grabbing him violently.

"What were you trying to do?" the second guard asked it.

The doppelgänger didn't reply.

Meanwhile, I slipped past them to where the real Matt should be, although he was as invisible to me as he was to the guards. I reached out and felt his shoulders.

"It's me, Missy," I whispered toward where his ear should be. "We're going on a brief excursion."

While the guards pushed the doppelgänger into the prison van, Matt and I descended the stairs at the end of the dock, and I led him to my car.

"What the heck just happened?" he asked.

"I'll explain when we're out of here."

"Why can't I see you? Or myself?"

"Remember how I mentioned before that I wanted to learn an invisibility spell?"

"Wow. You did it. And why was there a cloned me going into the van?"

"That's your doppelgänger."

"So, technically, I'm an escaped prisoner."

"Yes. But no one will realize that while they have your doppelgänger."

"You make it sound like it's temporary."

"It is. The doppelgänger was created by a demon and will fade away at some point."

"A demon? Are you talking about black magic?"

"Yes. This is your black-magic excursion. I hope it's fun."

We reached my car and got inside. As much as I would've preferred to stay invisible until after we left the medical campus, my car would look strange driving around with no one inside. So, I released the spell for both of us.

Though gaunt, unshaven, and looking scared, Matt was gorgeous to me. I gave him a big kiss.

"This is better than you seeing me in the jail visitation room," Matt said. "Um, can you take the handcuffs and shackles off me?"

"Of course."

I used my unlocking spell to unlock the devices. It took a few minutes, but once they were removed, Matt sighed with relief.

"I'm going to hide these in the trunk," I said, "in case we need them later."

"Need them for what? Do you have kinky games in mind?"

"No. In case we need them for when you return to jail."

"Oh." He was crestfallen.

"I owe you an explanation."

So, as we drove toward town, I narrated the entire story, from Ruth's testing of me with tasks, to the magic I used. I explained the point of it all: to allow me to join the coven so Ruth wouldn't kill me and to allow me to spy on her, eventually bringing her down.

"You're saying I'm just an achievement badge?" Matt asked.

"Yes. I'm sorry, but I hope you understand."

"And I really have to go back to jail after I'm presented to your mother?"

"Yes. But I'm very tempted to keep you with me. Maybe, I can convince the demon to keep the doppelgänger going."

Matt stared ahead grimly. His brief excitement at being free had completely disappeared.

"As soon as my doppelgänger disappears, I'm going to be considered an escaped prisoner. I'll have to be on the run forever, in danger of being shot and killed at any moment."

"Unless we keep the doppelgänger alive."

"But I'd still have to stay in hiding. I'd have to move somewhere else where no one would recognize me, change my name, and start a new life."

"Not if you're exonerated, and the murder charge is dropped," I said, taking a hand off the wheel and stroking his arm.

Matt shook his head. "Can the doppelgänger speak intelligently if Shortle wants to interrogate me again? Of if I make a

213

court appearance? This isn't going to work. We'll have to stick with the original plan and put me back in jail."

He was right. My brief fantasy of keeping him free and with me evaporated. Too bad getting him back into jail could be harder than getting him out.

"I must be the first person in the world who wants to go back to jail," Matt said.

"The food must be better than they say."

"No, it's not. But I want to do this right and clear my name."

"Are you angry with me for using you like this to advance my agenda with Ruth? This was her idea, remember?"

"I'm not sure how I feel. This all has been so weird."

I drove us straight to downtown Jellyfish Beach and parked outside of Ruth's apartment building. As always, just being near this building gave me a sense of dread in the pit of my stomach.

"Wait in the car," I said. "I'll go up and bring her down to see you here, so then we can just leave."

"What if I escape a second time today?"

"All the power to you."

I took the elevator to her floor, and Federico answered the door. He was wearing a leotard again. I didn't ask why.

"Saint Ruthless is in a meeting right now, but you can wait for her."

The furniture had been returned to the room, and the man pointed me toward the chairs facing the TV. A familiar woman sat on the couch in a stupor and stared at a game show on the screen.

I sat in the chair farthest from her and looked around.

A loud argument came from a bedroom, but I couldn't

make out what was said. I could tell only that it involved a man, and the other voice sounded like Ruth's. This went on for a while, and I tapped my feet nervously as I waited, just wanting to get this over with.

After Matt and I left, I would buy him lunch, and we'd hang out. I fantasized about what we would do for the rest of the afternoon, like lovers trying to get every drop out of their time together before the soldier went off to war.

The man's shouting got louder, then suddenly came a painful yelp that made me jump. The man screamed in agony. This was extremely disturbing, but the woman on the couch continued to watch TV, oblivious to the drama.

Should I help the man?

A door opened. And Fred Furman appeared in the living room, his face pale and sweaty. He was shocked to see me, but looked away as if he didn't know me.

He limped out of the apartment without a word.

Ruth walked into the room.

"Oh, it's you," she said. "Any news for me?"

"I got Matt out of jail."

"Excellent," she said with a super-villain smile. "Where is he?"

"In my car. Come down and you can see him."

"No, no, no. That wouldn't be proper. If you have a trophy for me, you must bring it to my place and present it to me."

"Matt's a he, not an it."

"This is all about protocol. Your task is not complete until you deliver him to my door. He can fit in the elevator, unlike the centaur."

I huffed in exasperation and got up. "I'll be right back."

Matt seemed puzzled when I opened the passenger door.

"Sorry," I said. "She wants you to come upstairs. It's all performative. She wants us to jump through another hoop for her ego."

"That's okay. I was getting nervous sitting here, worrying a cop would come by and recognize me."

He got out of the car, and we walked into the building.

"I'm going to buy you lunch after this," I said on the elevator. "It's the least I can do."

"One could argue that engineering my escape was the greatest thing you could do for me. But it turns out it's not so great."

"I'll make it up to you somehow. Once this is all over."

"You sound awfully optimistic given that your prime suspect, Umber, was killed."

"It doesn't matter. They'll probably drop the charges on you any minute now."

I didn't mention my suspicions of Shortle. If she was the culprit, she had every reason to keep the spotlight on Matt.

Federico let us into the apartment. Ruth stood at the far end of the living room in front of the TV, which had been turned off. Three acolytes I hadn't seen earlier were kneeling alongside the TV woman behind Ruth, facing us. Federico joined them.

"Hi," Matt said, giving a little wave.

"Followers, observe my power and influence," Ruth said pompously. "Under my orders, Missy used magic to free this man from jail. You may applaud now."

The acolytes clapped. It was rather lame compared to when she had the full coven here.

"Come prostrate yourselves before me," Ruth ordered Matt and me.

I didn't want to. I glanced at him, but he just shrugged and walked up to her, getting on his knees. His time in jail must have broken his spirit.

I joined him, on my knees, on the floor, beside him.

"Good work, Missy. We will induct you into the coven soon. Meanwhile, Matt will remain here as my slave."

CHAPTER 22
PUPPETEER

"Um, no offense, but I can't be your slave," Matt said to Ruth. "I'm supposed to be in jail right now. I need to get back before my doppelgänger fades away and the cops come looking for me."

"If the cops come looking for you, what can you do but hide?" she asked with a manic grin. "You might as well hide where they'll never expect you to be. Which is here. You'll be confined to my apartment. As my slave."

I couldn't believe I fell for her treachery again after what had happened with Trevor.

"Ruth, you never told me you'd make him a slave," I said. "You said all I needed to do was to show him to you to prove I'd broken him out."

"First, you must address me as Saint Ruthless. Second, I have every right to be . . . what's the word? Fickle. As a saint—goddess, really—I can be fickler than anyone. Your common human logic can't begin to understand me."

"We had a deal."

"There was no deal. I gave you a task, and you performed it."

"Don't I get a say in this?" Matt asked. "I don't want to be a slave. Heck, I'd rather be a prisoner in jail. I'm too headstrong. You'd find I would perform terribly as a slave. I'd be a huge disappointment."

"Federico?" Ruth said.

"Yes, your holiness?" replied her rotund manservant.

"How do you enjoy being my slave?"

"It is the greatest honor. I am fulfilling my destiny."

"This is ridiculous," I said. "Come on, Matt. We're leaving."

Before I even took a step, I learned that Ruth's immobility spell was different from mine. Painfully different. While mine turned a person into a living statue, hers was a binding spell. The sensation of tight ropes prevented my arms and legs from moving. It was like torture, which, I guess, was the point of black magic.

Matt was immobile, too. Something told me we would not have the intimate lunch I had planned.

"Why are you doing this to us? I've completed all the tasks you've given me. Please let us go," I pleaded, relieved that the spell hadn't affected my ability to speak.

"Did I say I was finished assigning tasks? Nope. You are supposed to prove your loyalty to me, and I don't feel convinced."

"Why not?"

"We've been enemies too long for me to trust you so easily."

"What do you mean, 'so easily'? I freed Matt from jail. That's like the hardest task in the world."

"You know what would be harder? Giving me your boyfriend to be my slave."

"He's not my boyfriend."

"I almost was," Matt said. "I don't think I'm interested anymore."

"Boyfriends are meant to be manipulated," Ruth said. "Like puppets."

She held her hands out and moved them. Matt's limbs jerked back and forth as if they were attached to strings.

"Dance, boyfriend!"

She motioned with her hands like a concert conductor, and Matt danced an awkward jig.

"Stop it," I said, trying to hold back my anger.

"I should teach you to dance, too."

I found myself doing a sloppy tap dance. It felt as if the ropes that bound me were suspending me in the air and controlling every movement of my legs and feet like a marionette.

As I danced, I was pulled closer to Matt, who dangled above the floor, his toes barely touching it.

"Show your boyfriend some affection," Ruth said with an evil grin.

My right arm was pulled backward, then yanked forward, my open palm smacking Matt on the butt.

Ruth chortled with delight. She was having a great time. None of her acolytes so much as smiled.

I had no choice but to fight back. Trying to decide which spell to use, I gathered my internal energies. But when I tried to access energy from the elements, I felt nothing. It was as if my connections were blocked.

Here in Ruth's lair, amid her black magic, I was sealed off from the world. And from sanity.

My power charm was inaccessible to me because I couldn't move my hand into my pocket to touch the charm. All I had were my internal energies. Everyone has these, but being born with the magic gene allowed me to control my energies and make them more powerful over the years.

As my knowledge of magic grew with time, so did my inherent power. Anyone can learn spells and memorize incantations, but only a true, natural witch has the power to alter the physical world with those spells.

The lesson Ruth had been trying to hammer home was that I would eventually reach the upper limit of my inherent power. The only way to go beyond my limit would be to accept black magic.

Accept the power of demons and darkness, of negation and nothingness. Of evil.

I had already crossed the line by using black magic to create Matt's doppelgänger. Doing so once, I believed, was harmless. I didn't want to cross over to the dark side again.

Without access to elemental energies while I was in Ruth's lair, I could use my own energies to negate her binding spell by meticulously taking it apart. But she would only attack me with another spell.

I needed to go on the offensive, though my arsenal of attack spells was piteously limited.

Keep it simple, stupid.

I probed Ruth, while she made Matt dance across her living room, to see what magic was brewing in her. She was so focused on humiliating Matt and me that she hadn't cast any protective spells around herself. She was overly confident that the wings of my magic would be clipped inside her apartment.

She was wrong.

A couple of minutes later, her chin dropped to her chest, and she was snoring like a drunken sumo wrestler. My little ol' sleep spell had done the trick.

I then cast a negation to dissolve the rest of her fading binding spell.

"Let's get the heck out of here before she wakes up," I said to Matt.

Ruth's acolytes were stirring. They must have been so accustomed to being passive that they were unsure what they were supposed to do when her prey attempted to escape.

Federico figured it out. He moved his large leotard-clad body to block the door.

"Really?" Matt said to him as we tried to leave. "You wouldn't last a minute in the county jail."

Matt hit him in the jaw with an elbow uppercut, followed by a gut punch. Federico doubled over, and Matt pushed him out of the way. We escaped from the apartment and ran down the stairs to my car.

"I think you should return me to the jail now," Matt said as I sped away from Ruth's building.

"Are you sure? We could hang out for a while."

"That evil woman is going to come after us. I'll be safer in jail."

"That's debatable."

"And what if she has a way to deactivate the doppelgänger right away? I'll be considered an escapee."

He had a point. Even though I was the one who had

conjured the doppelgänger, with the help of Asmodeus, Ruth's mastery of black magic might allow her to negate the spell whenever she wanted.

"Okay," I said. "If your doppelgänger is there when you return, you need to smother him with your presence."

"Huh?"

"Though he has a physicality you can touch, he's really just an apparition. I'll command him to self-destruct. But if he's still there, sit on him, lie on him, push yourself into him. Basically, absorb him back into your being. That should make him disappear for good."

"Won't that look odd to anyone watching?"

"At first, but they'll just think they have double vision."

"And how the heck do we get inside the jail?"

"Not we. You. You're going to be invisible."

"Why is it I don't feel reassured?"

"Because you worry too much."

He didn't need to worry, because I was worrying enough for the both of us.

My plan was simple. I drove us to the jail and parked in the visitors' lot, as far from obvious surveillance cameras as I could get. Then I cast my new invisibility spell, first on him, then on me.

"Okay," I said. "Let's go."

"We're just going to walk right in?"

"We'll wait for a new prisoner to arrive, and you'll slip inside with them. Just don't bump into anyone."

"I worked up a sweat when your mother was making me dance around. Can anyone smell me?"

I leaned closer to where he should be in the passenger seat and sniffed.

"Nope."

We walked through the parking lot toward the gloomy, formidable structure. The intake center was in a separate wing apart from the five-story building with the tiny windows that belonged to the cells. We stood in the shadows of the gate. I was worried that we might have to wait a while, although the jail handled all the prisoners in Crab County after their arrests and through their trials. There were several communities in this county.

And, apparently, several lawbreakers. Before long, a Crab County Sheriff's Department car with a man in the back seat pulled up to the gate. The deputy in the driver's seat spoke to a guard, and the gate rolled open.

"Good luck," I whispered to Matt. I gave him an air kiss because my lips missed their target. "I'll wait for two hours before I release your invisibility spell, to give you time to return to your cell."

"What if my bay is in lockdown? Give me four hours to be safe."

I felt his presence leave me as he followed the car through the gate. Soon after, it slid shut.

And Matt was gone from me again.

I needed to be close enough to the jail for my magic to reach him when I released the spell, so I killed time for four hours in my car, remaining invisible to avoid arousing suspicion. It was the longest four hours of my life, missing Matt already, and feeling guilty for what I'd done.

What kind of friend was I to break him out of jail and put him back inside?

All this trouble to ingratiate myself with Ruth so I could spy on her coven. And she betrayed me.

I knew she still wanted me to join, though. And she surely realized I was furious at her. She had threatened to kill me if I didn't join, then put me through these ridiculous tasks. If she truly wanted me to join, she couldn't push me any further.

What a mess I'd made of things. I'd worked so hard to find the murderer and exonerate Matt, yet my prime suspect was dead and seemingly innocent. I didn't know if he'd been killed by the drug runners or by a cop I once trusted and who, by all appearances, had gone rogue.

Worst of all, here Matt was, back in jail. His hopes for being exonerated were so dim that he willingly returned to his confinement.

I checked my watch. Four hours had passed. Hopefully, he was lingering invisibly near his cell, so that when I released the invisibility spell, he could slip back into his normal jail life, with no one noticing anything strange. And the doppelgänger would fade away with no complications.

I released the spell.

Then, I said aloud, "Depart, Doppelgänger," clapping my hands and reopening the knife wound.

It was all up to Matt to return to life as a prisoner. If there was a problem, I could do nothing about it now.

THE SUN WAS SETTING when I pulled into my driveway. What a day it had been, between absconding with Matt, fighting with Ruth, and then returning Matt. I'd conjured and expelled more magic in twelve hours than I normally did in a month.

When I went inside my house, I was greeted by two hungry cats and a ravenous lizard. It was amusing to see my witch's familiar, with human intelligence, scampering about my feet just like one of my pets.

Not only had I let down Matt, but my other loved ones—those with fur and scales—had been neglected, too.

The same was true with my day job. With all that was going on, I'd fallen short of the hours I should have been at the botanica. Thank heavens Luisa was tolerant of my crazy life.

After I opened two cans of wet food for the cats and poured a bowl of iguana chow for Tony, I went into my bedroom to take off my clothes and take a warm bath.

But something unseen was rattling around on the floor. At first, I worried it was a large beetle or cockroach, but the sound it made on my hardwood floor was that of a small stone or pebble.

Then, I remembered the fossilized tooth the sprite chieftain had lent me. It wasn't on my dresser where I'd left it. I bent down and saw the tooth bouncing around on the floor beneath the dresser it had fallen from.

Grabbing it, I was immediately overcome by the emotions of anger and fear so powerful they had shattered the sprites' field of psychic energy.

I wasn't sure how I knew this, but two sprites were in a fight to the death.

CHAPTER 23
SPRITE FIGHT

When I grasped the magic tooth, I left my body and flew above the night-cloaked city as fast as a rocket. Soon, I soared over the neighboring town that was in Luna's territory. When I reached the farthest suburbs, I slowed and descended until I hovered above a large parcel of green land, a nature preserve.

I dropped in altitude until I was flying just above the ground over a walking path of sugary white sand that reflected the moonlight. I followed the winding path through sabal palms, longleaf pines, and gumbo limbo trees. Beside the trail was a small clearing with a burrow in the sand made by a gopher tortoise.

My consciousness slipped into the hole without hesitation.

If I were in my physical body, I would never choose to go into a gopher tortoise burrow, even if I could fit into the opening made by the large reptile. Aside from the tortoises, other creatures made their homes in the burrows, including rattlesnakes.

And, I assumed, crested mouth sprites.

But enter the hole I did, because I had no choice. I was just being taken along for the ride.

I saw no rattlesnakes or tortoises, but after the burrow wound deeper into the earth, it ended at a wall of rock. My consciousness slipped through a cleft in the rock.

Beneath the sand of South Florida is a shelf of limestone, filled with innumerable subterranean pockets, such as the cave-like space I just entered. Though it was as dark as pitch, I could see in here.

It appeared to be a nest, with a bed made of straw and human teeth scattered about.

And just past the bed, mortal combat was taking place.

Rachel and Luna fought like wolves. Unable to fly in the confined space, they wrestled on the stone floor, biting and scratching each other.

"Stop it!" I tried to shout, but no words came from me.

"Get out of my nest!" Luna screamed.

"It's mine now," replied Rachel, her words coming in short staccato bursts between punches. "You don't deserve it. You live like a glutton, with more teeth than any sprite could need. There are so many you don't even harvest them all and let them go to waste. You're a lazy, slothful pig—not a sprite. You don't deserve to live."

Rachel had pinned Luna to the floor with her hands wrapped around her rival's throat.

A murder was about to ensue, and I had to stop it, but I wasn't in my corporeal form. Even if I returned to my body and drove to this nature preserve in time, I couldn't help Luna. And even if I managed to find the exact burrow, I couldn't fit into it, especially not in the limestone pocket where the nest was.

I didn't know what to do other than cry out in my mind to Chieftain Lady Boldfly. I called out to Mrs. Lupis and Mr. Lopez, too, though only the chieftain would be able to get into this place. But my two handlers always seemed to know what I was up to, and they could summon the chieftain if I wasn't able to.

Luna squirmed frantically, trying to get out from beneath Rachel. But she was weakening, her face turning purple with her attacker's claw-like hands squeezing her neck.

I shouted at Rachel again to stop, but she didn't hear me. I thrust my consciousness against her, ramming her, but I passed right through her like a ghost.

Luna had passed out. I despaired she was about to die. Suddenly, a moaning came from the fissure I had used to enter this cave. Air blew through it, increasing in intensity and noise, as if a cyclone was pushing through the tortoise's burrow.

The unending blast of wind blew Luna's nest apart, scattering the straw about the cave. It looked like the transparent dust container of a vacuum cleaner in here, with straw and teeth blowing in circles around the limestone cavity.

Rachel joined the debris, bouncing around like a rag doll. My heart surged with hope as I studied Luna lying on the floor, hoping to see signs of her breathing again.

But suddenly, I was back in my bedroom, standing beside my dresser with the fossilized tooth burning in my hand. I felt completely disoriented.

My doorbell rang. I knew exactly who it was at my door.

Mrs. Lupis and Mr. Lopez stood there with grim expressions.

"Come," Mrs. Lupis said. "We must do an extraction."

"A tooth fairy extraction," said Mr. Lopez.

"Isn't that what Angela is supposed to do?"

"She's busy right now," Mr. Lopez replied. "An issue with a beached mermaid. Please drive us right away to the Sandspur Natural Area on Citrus Road in Sailfish Beach."

"Don't you guys have a car?" I asked.

"No."

"How do you get around?"

"We find a way."

I would serve as their way tonight.

The preserve was not open at this late hour, of course, and the gates to the parking lot were closed. So, I parked on the grassy roadside nearby. I followed Mrs. Lupis and Mr. Lopez as they ducked under the gate arm and into the parking lot. They behaved as if they knew where they were going, though how they would find the exact tortoise burrow was beyond me.

However, standing in human form at the head of the hiking trail, was the chieftain and two additional sprites behind her. The two held Rachel, in her natural sprite form, tied up with ropes. Being bound would prevent her from shifting to a larger human body.

"Thank you for taking her off our hands," the chieftain said. "Our population is too small and spread out to make a detention center feasible."

"It's our pleasure," Mr. Lopez said with a smile. "We've wanted to study a crested mouth sprite for quite some time."

"You're not doing anything to me," Rachel said.

"Is Luna okay?" I asked.

"She is receiving care and should recover nicely," the chieftain replied. "Thank you for alerting me of her peril."

"I'm so happy you saved her, because I couldn't."

"Murder is unheard of among our species. We can't afford to lose any of our members. Except for," the chieftain turned and glared at Rachel, "psychotic sprites."

"Luna doesn't deserve this territory," Rachel said. "It's too big for her, and my territory is too small. It's an injustice, and I was only trying to correct it."

"You can believe what you want, but you have no right to be here. Even I, as chieftain, can't mete out punishment on my own. The entire council had to be convened."

"And they did nothing?"

"Oh, they did. Take her away now," the chieftain said to my handlers. "She has been banished from our species for life."

Mrs. Lupis picked up Rachel and held her as she would a baby, until the psycho sprite began thrashing about like a caught fish. Mrs. Lupis then grabbed her by her feet and carried her upside down to my car, dumping her in the trunk.

We said our goodbyes to the sprites, and I drove toward the hidden location of the Society's Cryptid Sanctuary. I knew the way from a previous visit.

"Doesn't the Society have enough money to give you guys a company car?" I asked, more for making small talk than in the expectation of a transparent answer.

"You can't get driver's licenses when you're not human," Mr. Lopez said.

They'd let it slip before that the two of them were considered cryptids, but they'd never told me what species they were. I'd always felt too uncomfortable to ask.

"No one can tell you're not human," I said. "You could easily fool the folks at the DMV."

"There are other complicating factors."

He didn't elaborate, and I left it at that.

I almost missed the dirt road leading to the sanctuary since it was the dead of night, and no streetlamps were nearby. The road was also hemmed in by underbrush.

Everyone in the car was silent as we rolled slowly along the rough road. The only sound was the furious buzzing of Rachel's insect-like wings in the trunk. But she wasn't going to fly anywhere.

The road ended at a shallow creek, and I had to overcome my instinct to stop. I descended the creek bank and drove through the water. On the opposite bank was a tall wall of sawgrass, blocking all views, but I kept driving, and the wall magically parted to allow the car through on a continuation of the dirt road through the tall grass.

The gate ahead automatically swung open, and we entered the sanctuary that looked like a cross between a luxury resort and a college campus. The property somehow existed in a parallel universe and was completely invisible to anyone traveling through or above the surrounding wilderness of a national wildlife preserve.

"You can let us off at the visitors' center," Mrs. Lupis said.

I pulled up at the building that looked like a facility busloads of kids on field trips would throng into. But did this place ever get visitors?

Mr. Lopez and Mrs. Lupis got out of my car, the latter opening the trunk to collect their sprite prisoner.

"You can go home now," Mr. Lopez said. "We'll be just fine. Thanks for your help."

I drove home exhausted, wondering when a replacement sprite would be appointed to serve as the new tooth fairy for Jellyfish Beach. But thoughts of sprites faded when I got home. I devoured a grilled cheese sandwich before falling into bed, delaying my collapse onto the mattress just long enough to allow the cats to scamper to safety.

Then, the phone rang. The robotic voice asked me to accept a call from the Crab County Jail. Of course, I said yes.

"Matt! Are you okay? Did you make it back without being caught?"

"Yeah. I'm back. My cellmate didn't even notice I'd been gone, since I don't like to talk to him, and my doppelgänger didn't talk at all. The invisibility spell went away at the perfect time, when everyone was walking back from the mess hall. But getting rid of the doppelgänger was a bit dicey. As I crushed myself into my duplicate, my cellmate thought he was having a stroke that caused him to see double."

"I'm so glad you're good now."

"I'm not good," Matt said dourly. "I'm in jail."

"Of course. But you're safe."

"I'm safe until someone sticks a shiv in my back."

"I meant you're safe from being classified as an escapee." I didn't like the way this conversation was going.

"You actually abducted me from custody, then made me return to jail."

"I didn't make you return. Matt, we've already discussed this."

"Not that my time free was much fun. Being tortured by your mother wasn't a walk in the park."

"But you enjoyed spending time with me, right?"

"Of course. For the few minutes we had. And now, I'm here with a bunch of carjackers and burglars who all smell horrible."

"It will end soon," I said in the calming voice I had used as a nurse. "Our justice system is far from perfect, but you're totally innocent. And you will be freed."

The robotic voice announced our time was running out, and Matt said goodnight in a pouty voice.

The truth was, I didn't have as much faith in him being freed as I had pretended. Which made it really weird when I turned on the TV to relax after the tense phone call.

The 11:00 p.m. local news was on. And Detective Shortle was standing behind a podium between the police chief and a Drug Enforcement Agency officer.

"Thanks to the superb work of Detective Cindy Shortle," the chief said, "we made an arrest tonight of suspected Colombian drug lord Felix Carrascal. He's being charged with ordering the murder of one of his smugglers, Burt Umber."

CHAPTER 24

NEW SPRITE IN TOWN

I sat transfixed, watching the televised news conference.

The chief of police did most of the talking, describing how Carrascal had been a thorn in the side of law enforcement. Authorities had arrested him months ago for drug smuggling after the kingpin moved his operation from the Miami area to the small community of Jellyfish Beach, where he had a vacation home. I hadn't realized a mansion could be considered a vacation home.

Thanks to complex legal maneuvering by the drug lord's expensive lawyers, not to mention the unfortunate prevalence of witnesses disappearing or showing up dead, a trial still hadn't begun. It was seemingly impossible to bring Carrascal to justice.

The ambitious young detective Cindy Shortle (those were the chief's exact words) took it upon herself to investigate the suspect. When yet another witness, Burt Umber, was murdered, the Jellyfish Beach Police Department sprang to action.

Shortle tried to suppress a smile. The DEA agent glowered. After all, his agency was probably at fault for failing to put Carrascal in prison.

"Thank you for your kind words," Shortle said to the chief after he motioned for her to take over the podium. She said a bunch of pablum, giving credit to the various agencies involved, including the DEA, then added a comment.

"Anyone who knew Burt Umber, please come speak with us. Your help is crucial for our investigation."

I took this as a sign that my theory was correct: Burt Umber was the serial murderer after all. My truth spell must have failed with him. But I wanted confirmation. The next day, when the botanica was devoid of customers, I called the detective. Surprisingly, she took my call.

"Congratulations on nailing Carrascal," I said. "I don't like people shooting at my house and killing someone, even if the someone was an intruder who would have harmed me."

"I know you were suspicious that I shot Umber," Shortle said.

"Me? Never."

"Yes, you were. You thought I was a rogue cop."

Anger stirred in me. "You believe Matt Rosen is a rogue journalist!"

"You should know that I took the information you gathered about Umber very seriously. The chief wants to pin all the murders on Carrascal's hitmen, but Chubb's death doesn't fit in. I believe you were right: Umber killed Puttle and Oddbelly because they witnessed his drug running. He killed Chubb because of bad blood over his wife. I think the confession you got from Oddbelly, that he killed Jacobs, was legit."

"I'm glad you believed me."

"So, I reached out to Umber before he was killed. I made it seem like I was looking for connections between him and Carrascal, but I was also probing him about the murders. It looks as though Umber's boss was worried he would become an informant."

It didn't help that I had mentioned Umber to Carrascal, too. I decided not to bring up that fact to Shortle.

"Do you think Carrascal will wriggle out of trouble again?" I asked.

"We arrested someone we believe was the hitman who took out Umber. If we can convince him to flip, we can nail Carrascal to the wall for Umber's murder. Then, with the DEA, we'll build a stronger case against him for narcotics."

"What about the other murders? When will you blame them on Umber?"

"The assistant state attorney is almost there. I just need to push him a bit further. He's already agreed to drop the one charge and the other pending charges against your pal, Rosen."

A thrill swept through me. "For real?"

"For real. They're processing his release as we speak."

I actually got a little teary-eyed. Fortunately, since this was a phone call, Shortle wouldn't know.

"Thank you, Detective."

"If you turn up any additional evidence on Umber, let me know," she said before hanging up.

She respected my investigations and asked me for help. It was an additional boost to my celebratory mood.

The icing on the cake would be to hear from Matt. But the day went by, and I didn't. He was probably still being processed for release. Or, he was out, but his phone battery was dead. I kept waiting for my phone to ring or for him to show up at the botanica. It didn't happen.

Not long after I got home, my doorbell rang. My heart surged—it was Matt!

Nope. It was Mrs. Lupis and Mr. Lopez. With them was a pretty, petite woman with auburn hair.

"We'd like you to meet the new tooth fairy in town," Mrs. Lupis said with a rare smile. "Aurora, meet Missy Mindle."

"Welcome to our humble city," I said, shaking her delicate hand. In human form, she had nothing to suggest she was, in reality, a crested mouth sprite.

"We thought you deserved an introduction after all you've been through," Mr. Lopez said to me.

"It's a pleasure to meet you," Aurora said in a squeaky voice. Her voice was the one thing that gave her away as a sprite in human form.

"Please, everyone, come inside."

"There's no time, I'm afraid," Aurora said. "I have a tooth visit to make tonight, and I want to be sure I find the correct address. I'm new at this job, and I want to get it right."

"Of course. How, then, have you been getting the energy you need if you haven't touched teeth?"

"From my family. But it was time I left the nest!" she said with a perky smile. "It's such an honor to become a tooth fairy."

"Of course."

"I mean, that human parents trust me enough to enter their homes, even if they don't realize a tooth fairy is literally entering their homes. They think I'm just a cute piece of folklore."

"To be honest," I said, "so did I, until recently."

"I was trained to be honorable and trustworthy with the innocent children I visit. And I must always be accepting and non-judgmental of the homes I enter."

"What do you mean?"

"Some parents are rich, and others are poor. Some are messy, while many are tidy. I might see evidence of bad parenting, but it is not my place to judge."

"What if you find evidence of a child being mistreated or in danger?"

"A tooth fairy does not intervene. I can pass such information on to our chieftain, and she can inform human authorities if she decides that is needed. But a tooth fairy never intervenes. We come and go unseen and unheard. We leave no trace that we were there. Unless the parents believe in the tooth fairy."

"There are parents who do?"

"That's what I was told, though they are very rare. In such a case, I take the tooth and leave money. Otherwise, the parents do that after I have fed upon the tooth's energy."

"You sound very well trained," I said. "You'll do an excellent job."

After my visitors left, I went about my evening glued to my phone. When would Matt call me? Or maybe he'd come by?

But what if there was a bureaucratic breakdown, and he hadn't even been released yet? I was going crazy.

Finally, as it neared my bedtime, I broke down and called him, not expecting his phone to be working.

"Hey," he said. "I'm out and back in my bungalow. My heartbeat is back to normal, by the way."

"How did you get home? I would have been happy to give you a ride."

"No problem. I took a ride share. I didn't want to bother you."

"It wouldn't have been a bother."

"I figured you'd be busy with your coven."

"Surely, you remember our recent encounter with Ruth. I have not been accepted into the coven."

"You will. After all, you've tried so hard to be."

"Okay, I understand you feel used."

"Used? Being abducted from my guards, abused by your mother, and then forced to sneak back into that hellish place called jail—all because your mommy wanted you to jump through hoops. That's being used?"

"Your sarcasm is well-deserved. I apologize for using you like that. It's just very important for me to destroy Ruth, or at least to get her to move away. Joining the coven and fighting her from within is the best way. It's the only way."

"I don't care about your mother."

"Stop calling her my mother."

"You need to step back and look at this objectively. It's obvious that you've got a mother-daughter rivalry going on."

"Nonsense. She's dangerous. Not just for me, but for all of Jellyfish Beach."

"I think you also have an unhealthy fascination with black magic. That's why you're so eager to join her cult. You know that black magic can expand your powers."

240

"That's not true!" Deep down, I worried it was true, so his claim was making me furious.

"If you want to punish me for obeying Ruth and using you, go right ahead. I deserve it. But don't you dare pretend that she isn't a big threat to this town—to magic practitioners, to the werewolves, to everyone."

"So says the person who broke me out of jail."

"Listen, mister, my investigating is what helped get your charges dropped. Shortle even said as much."

"Yeah, right."

"I was homing in on Umber as the killer, and she said she agrees with me. Carrascal has been indicted for ordering his murder."

"What's this?"

I explained the big news he missed while cut off from the world.

"Umber killed those people to eliminate witnesses to his drug smuggling. He killed Chubb because of a fight over his wife. Carrascal had Umber killed because he was bringing scrutiny to Carrascal. Which was partly my fault, I guess. The big prize would be if we could prove that Carrascal ordered Umber to kill any of his victims. Which would be another reason Carrascal would want him eliminated."

Matt was silent. I knew my words were having the same effect on him as chum has on sharks. Could he resist getting involved in this story?

"You've done a great job with this investigation, Missy," he said. "And I'm not being sarcastic. I think you should continue."

"Don't you want to sink your teeth into it?"

"No. I need to get back into my employer's good graces. They put out some statements defending me and press freedom. They even picked up my legal fees after I was arrested. But I know they weren't thrilled to have a senior reporter jailed for murder. I have a lot of repair work to do if I want to keep my job."

"Yeah, by writing about the actual murderer."

He was silent again.

"Maybe. Just give me a little space right now. I need to adjust to life on the outside. And you should know, I'm very grateful that you paid Paul's fees in the beginning and covered my expenses in jail."

"It was the least I could do."

I was tempted to remind him that he hadn't been in jail for very long, but I wisely kept my mouth shut.

We agreed we'd talk again soon and said goodnight. I lay in bed for hours, unable to sleep, aching with guilt for what I'd made him go through.

But it hadn't been my fault he'd been arrested in the first place. That was the fault of Shortle and the state attorney's office. And it was because of Matt's bad luck to have written articles critical of the victims before they were killed, and even had verbal conflicts with two of them.

Matt had crossed the line from being objective to judgmental when he publicly lit into a few of them. It was no wonder they believed he would intervene to punish the victims, who were, I admit, bad men.

Judgmental. Intervene. Where had I heard those words before?

From the mouth of the brand-new tooth fairy, the young,

crested mouth sprite. She had been correctly taught to keep her opinions to herself when encountering negligent parents.

Unlike her predecessor, Rachel. Boy, was she a mess. Mouthing off about the homes she'd visited and then taking matters into her own hands with her rival, Luna.

She had been too judgmental and had crossed the line.

Something nagged at my mind like a kid tugging at my sleeve.

The victims were all parents, weren't they?

My heart started racing, and I realized I would not get any sleep tonight.

CHAPTER 25
GOING DENTAL

Yes, I knew all the victims had been parents, except, perhaps, the shark fisherman strangled by Oddbelly. The first victim, Puttle, definitely was, because he killed a tooth fairy who had visited his son.

How old were the other victims' kids?

The only way I could take a guess at that was to rely on the archives of Matt's employer, *The Jellyfish Beach Journal*. They still followed the old-school newspaper practice of publishing birth and death notices.

So, I searched for birth notices from approximately six to twelve years ago. The children born back then would now be at the age when they lost their baby teeth.

And the tooth fairy would make repeated visits to their homes, even past the point when they stopped believing in her. The visits would be opportunities to witness the conditions in which the children lived and how well they were treated.

Then, to make judgments and to mete out extra-judicial

punishments—if you were a psycho sprite. Executions carried out not with guns, but with more crude methods.

By a psycho sprite named Rachel.

It took me a couple of hours to find the birth records I sought, and I was fortunate that all the victims' children had been born in Jellyfish Beach.

They were now between six and twelve years old. The tooth-shedding ages.

It was reasonable to assume that Rachel had visited all of them.

First, she exacted vengeance on Jerome Puttle, who killed one of her kind—recklessly putting his son at risk. But what about the other victims? They weren't good men, but were they also guilty of transgressions that pushed Rachel over the edge?

I could search the newspaper archives, but what I really needed was help from a journalist.

When I called Matt, he feigned disinterest, but I could tell that my new theory intrigued him.

"We know Charles Chubb physically abused his wife," Matt said. "I don't know if their children witnessed the abuse, or if that was enough reason to kill him."

"Do you think he harmed the children?"

"If he did, the records might be sealed, but I'll look into it."

"And as for Billy Ray Jacobs," I said, "Shortle believes Todd Oddbelly's confession was legit, and that he did, in fact, strangle Jacobs. And I don't know if Jacobs had children. I didn't see any birth records associated with his name."

"Jacobs wasn't married, as far as I know. If he had any children, he didn't play an active role in their lives. Which leaves Oddbelly. He had a family."

"And a child of tooth-shedding age."

"I'll look into him."

"Thank you. I really appreciate it," I said in my sweetest, most sincere voice.

"I'm just helping you because this is an interesting angle. It doesn't mean we're investigative partners again."

"God forbid we would be that. Message received. You're tolerating my presence only out of curiosity."

"You were never this sarcastic when I first met you."

"I've grown a lot since then."

"I'll get back to you," he said, hanging up.

Later that day, while I was stocking shelves at the botanica, I had a small tinge of doubt. Was it really such a good idea to discover that a crested mouth sprite had murdered the men? Crimes by supernaturals against humans were one of the biggest concerns of the Friends of Cryptids Society.

Was I opening a giant can of worms?

After more contemplation, I decided it was worth any trouble we caused if, in fact, Rachel was the murderer. Achieving justice was critical to me. Having a blood relative like Ruth made me realize that without justice and accountability, we were all just monsters of the worst kind.

The Society had dealt with homicidal cryptids before, and they could do so again. What kind of penalty they would impose was up to them. My role was only to seek the truth.

Matt called me right after I had wound up the botanica's mystical grandfather clock, which was never to be allowed to run down lest the world end (long story), and was about to lock the store up for the night.

"Okay, I went through our archive and public court records,

as well as arrest reports," he said. "And I believe we have motives for the sprite to perform extrajudicial punishments of these men."

"Don't leave me waiting."

"Charles Chubb kidnapped his children from his wife after their divorce went through and she got custody."

"Oh my."

"He took them out of state and didn't allow them to go to school. He basically kept them as prisoners until law enforcement tracked him down. This happened fairly recently. For some reason, his wife didn't press charges."

"Shortle never said anything about it."

"She wasn't very good about sharing information, especially with me, who she was trying to railroad to prison."

I reminded myself that even though Shortle and I were on better terms now, I still couldn't trust her completely.

"What about Oddbelly?" I asked.

"He was cited several times for child neglect and reckless endangerment. He was stopped for driving under the influence while the kids were in the car and weren't wearing safety belts. On another occasion, he was arrested for leaving a young child in the car unsupervised while he was shopping. And there were other incidents."

"Would Rachel know about all these bad things that Chubb and Oddbelly did?"

"I don't exactly know how she would, but she is a supernatural creature, after all. You can ask your handlers from the Society."

"I will. I'll pass along this information to them, though I'm worried about the repercussions."

"That's their problem, not yours."

"But they always seem to get me involved in their problems."

As a supernatural creature, a crested mouth sprite would possess all sorts of abilities I couldn't even imagine, such as the capacity to learn about three fathers' endangerment of their children.

And have strength far beyond that of a human.

Still, one murder potentially had a witness, though none had admitted seeing the actual crime. I drove to the boat ramp in Port Inferno to see if he was around.

Sure enough, Larry was fishing at the pier beside the ramp.

"Haven't seen you for a while," he said to me.

"I've been busy, but I wanted to ask you something. Everyone believes that Burt Umber killed Jerome Puttle. Do you?"

"What's it matter what I think?"

"You found the body. I was thinking you could have been on your boat, checking your traps, when the murder took place."

"I didn't see anything."

"You saw my friend, who ended up getting arrested for the murder."

"I saw him after Puttle went into the drink."

"Did you see who put Puttle into the crab trap?"

"Everyone keeps asking me, but no. I didn't see it."

"You were out on the water at the time, right?"

"Not near enough to Puttle to see what happened."

He was trying to avoid my eyes, so he didn't notice when I sprinkled powder on his feet.

"I'm asking you again," I said. "What happened?"

He turned his head toward me, and his eyes had the glassy, eager look that said my truth spell had kicked in.

"What I saw didn't make any sense at all," he replied.

"Tell me more."

"I was on the other side of the inlet, but I could see Puttle working his traps. There was a large bird hovering over him. Though, it didn't really look like a bird. The wings were different. I don't know. This was really early and there wasn't much light."

"Tell me more."

"What happened next couldn't have happened. I must have been hallucinating. It was crazy."

"Go on."

"The bird turned into a human. A woman. It makes no sense, but that's what I saw. She was standing in the boat beating Puttle with an oar. And then . . . It was horrible. She tore open the top of a trap, picked him up, and squeezed him into it. She threw it overboard. It was near some of my traps because Puttle was stealing from them."

"Why didn't you tell this to the police?" I asked.

"Are you crazy? They'd put me away in the loony bin for a story like that. Besides, I'd be admitting I saw him stealing from my traps, and the cops would think I killed him and made up this crazy story. You think it's crazy, right?"

"Nope. I don't think it's crazy at all. But you might not want to tell anyone else. Not everyone is as open-minded as I am."

WHEN I GOT HOME—YOU guessed it—Mrs. Lupis and Mr. Lopez were waiting for me.

"You have some information for us?" they asked me in unison.

"Yeah. Crazy stuff. Come inside and have some tea. You'll need to be sitting down for this."

We all sat at my kitchen table, all three of us sipping cups of Earl Grey, while I summed up the entire story of my revelation that Rachel had been the murderer. I finished with Larry's eyewitness account.

The two looked at me stone faced.

"Would Rachel have been able to learn about the victims' offenses against their children?" I asked.

"Crested mouth sprites have advanced telepathic powers," Mr. Lopez said. "Rachel could have dug up that information from their memories even if they weren't thinking about it."

"As we've learned, she is terribly nosy and judgmental," his partner said.

"What are you going to do with what I've told you?"

"We should get her to confess," Mrs. Lupis said.

"Can I use my truth spell on her?"

They both shook their heads. "It won't work."

"What if she won't confess?"

"Based on our observations of her in captivity," said Mrs. Lupis, "she's prone to bragging. I believe she will gladly confess."

"Then what will you do to her?"

"The Society does not practice capital punishment. We only

put down creatures who are suffering or are a serious risk of harm to others. She will remain our guest for the rest of her lifespan."

"And how long is that?"

"Only a few hundred years. Mr. Lopez and I will personally ensure she's well cared for throughout the rest of her life."

"Oh. You mean you guys will live . . . Never mind."

"It's always so awkward talking about life expectancies with a human," Mr. Lopez said.

"It's like me talking about living a long life to a fruit fly."

"Exactly!" He beamed. "Perfect analogy!"

This was only making me more depressed.

"Please keep me updated if she confesses," I said.

"You're going with us to speak to her," said Mrs. Lupis.

"Because you need a ride to the sanctuary? I thought you guys had other means of travel."

"Because we believe you deserve to be there if we can put this case to rest."

"Until now, you've assumed the murders were committed by a human and were trying to exonerate your friend," Mr. Lopez said. "Believe it or not, the murders are of much greater importance than that, because cryptid-on-human violence is so rare nowadays. We may have led you to believe that the Society's mission is only cataloging and studying cryptids, but suppressing their interactions with humans is just as crucial."

"Yeah, I understand why that would be the case."

My handlers stood up at the same time and placed their empty teacups and saucers in my sink.

"Shall we go now?" they asked in unison.

It was late in the afternoon when we crossed from the

normal world into the alternate universe of the Cryptid Sanctuary, the setting sun piercing the thick sawgrass with tiny needles of light and creating a glow across the tops of the grass.

We arrived at a busy campus with daytime cryptids out enjoying the weather with human caretakers here and there among them. Two trolls strolled by us, carrying pickleball paddles. A griffin flew by and landed in a banyan tree.

But we were going inside a building that could only be described as a jail, though walking through the lobby, I felt like I was entering an undergraduate dorm at a college.

My handlers spoke to a man at the front desk who I assumed was human. He made a phone call, and a large, bald man in scrubs came out through a heavy security door.

"I am Sven," he said. "I will take you to the sprite. Follow me and don't engage with any of the cryptids we pass."

He held a key card to a panel beside the door, and we could hear several loud clicks as giant bolts slid aside. The door swung open, and we followed him through it.

We went down a long corridor lined with steel doors. At the end, we made a right into a corridor with plexiglass windows beside the doors. It was like passing through the reptile house at the zoo: behind each window was a unique environment, from jungle to desert, from aquarium to what looked like a hotel room.

In some environments, the occupants were invisible to my human eyes. In one room that looked like a forest, a Sasquatch stared at me and waved. Obeying the instructions I was given, I didn't wave back.

In another room, a woman popped up suddenly from below

the windowsill, startling me. When I saw that below her torso she had the body of a giant snake, I stifled a scream.

We turned into another hallway and stopped in front of a steel door. There was no window for this cell, only a small video screen that showed the room through a fisheye lens. I guess it was so we could see the occupant before the door was opened, to avoid ambushes.

Sven pressed his key card on the reader, and once again, we heard three bolts slide away.

He opened the door and said, "Rachel, you have visitors."

The room resembled Luna's cave at the end of the tortoise burrow. This one, too, had a large nest in the center made from woven grass. Rachel sat in it, in her natural sprite form, looking like she was reclining in a beanbag chair.

She glowered at us like a sulking child. "What do *you* want?"

Mrs. Lupis stepped closer to the nest, while the rest of us remained by the door. Sven came in and locked the door behind us, keeping his hand on a metal tube in a hip holster. I assumed it was some sort of taser, but probably magical.

"Rachel, it appears that you were a very busy sprite, aside from your tooth duties," Mrs. Lupis said.

"Yeah, I know," she replied in her street-tough voice. "I encroached on another sprite's territory. Big deal."

"And attacked her."

"She deserved it."

"Were any humans deserving of your punishment? Such as parents who neglected or endangered their children?"

"There were more than you want to know."

"Did you actually punish any of them?"

"I refrained, in spite of myself."

Mrs. Lupis stepped closer to the sprite, pointing at her aggressively. I felt a surge of magical energy in the room. But what kind of magic?

"I don't believe you refrained. Like you said, that would be against your nature. I believe you did what you thought was right, what the humans deserved."

Rachel jumped to her feet like a maniacal doll, then rose into the air, her bug-like wings buzzing.

"Yeah, I took out a few vermin," she said, cackling in a manner that sounded uncannily like my mother's famous evil cackle. "That's what those humans were—vermin."

"Did you kill Jerome Puttle?"

"The guy who shot my predecessor, only inches from his child's face? Yeah, I killed him. In a pretty funny way, don't cha think?"

"I didn't think it was funny, though it had a certain irony to it. What about Charles Chubb?"

"The wife beater? Yeah, I brained him with the replica of a mythological woman. Plenty of irony to that."

"Perhaps. What about Todd Oddbelly?"

"The guy was totally irresponsible and a danger to his children. When I found out he'd strangled his friend, I did the same to him using his tow truck's cable. Again, totally ironic."

"Did you kill any other humans in Jellyfish Beach?"

"Nope. I haven't had the chance. I just got here, after all. Before this, my territory was the theme parks in Orlando. Lots of young kids there, and often they'd lose a tooth during their vacation. Plenty of energy for me to feed upon. But their parents often misbehaved during their vacations, and my way of dealing with that got me banished by the Central Florida chieftain."

"Rachel, you told me when we first met that sprites don't kill humans," I said.

"They don't. I'm unique that way," she replied proudly.

Mr. Lopez had been videoing the interview. When his partner looked back at him, he nodded.

Mrs. Lupis waved her hand, and the magical energy dissipated from the room.

"I believe we have the information we need," she said to Rachel. "Be on your best behavior, and you'll continue to have all the teeth you need to stay healthy."

"Finally. It takes getting imprisoned to get the dental energy I need," Rachel replied. "Now, that's ironic."

It was time to leave. We moved toward the door, waiting for Sven to unlock it.

"The greatest irony of all," Rachel said in a low voice, "comes from you, witch. You act like you're moral and pure, but you've been dabbling in black magic, haven't you?"

She had just used her telepathy on me, I realized, as my body slammed into the concrete wall of the cell, and bony, human-sized fingers wrapped around my neck, pushing into my throat.

I snapped my head backward and hit Rachel in the face, stunning her just enough to allow me to squirm my body around to face her.

She was in human form, and her eyes blazed with fury while her oversized mouth leered like a homicidal clown's. Sven had his right forearm around her neck and the metal tube that I had assumed was a taser of some sort in his left hand.

Everywhere he touched her with it, purple sparks danced across her body.

The problem with providing Rachel with all the tooth energy she needed was readily apparent; she was stronger than an ox. This creature, who had stuffed a full-grown man into a crab trap, was planning to do something worse to me.

She bellowed and bent her body forward, flipping Sven upside down and slamming him into the wall beside me.

I jumped out of the way, retreating to the farthest part of the cell and casting a protection spell around myself. Mrs. Lupis and Mr. Lopez would have to fend for themselves, because I needed to concentrate all my magic on my safety while I somehow disabled Rachel.

My two handlers merely stood there, pointing at Rachel, sending forth their own form of magic that wasn't stopping the sprite.

Sven regained his feet and got Rachel in a bear hug, giving me the precious time I needed. But the sleep spell I cast upon her was not working.

Next, I tried my immobility spell, which was more powerful. It didn't work, either. I'd used both spells with success against supernaturals before, but this crested mouth sprite was impervious to them.

Rachel thrashed about like a tiger, and Sven flew across the room and landed in her nest. In her hand, she had his key card.

"Don't let her escape!" Mrs. Lupis shouted.

Rachel pressed the card against the lock panel, but I used my unlocking spell in reverse to prevent the bolts from sliding.

She turned to me, her mouth quivering with rage.

"You could have escaped death," she said in a low voice. "Now, you die."

Unfortunately, for Rachel, now I was invisible.

"Your clever little tricks won't stop me," she said. "I can smell exactly where you are."

She lunged at me. I danced out of the way. She tried again, and I evaded her easily.

Suddenly, she transformed into her natural sprite form, hovering near the ceiling of the cell.

"Finally, the magic worked," Mrs. Lupis said, at wit's end. "We use it against cryptids who can shift or camouflage themselves. It forces them to revert to their natural forms. I can't believe how much this sprite resisted it."

I think she was speaking to invisible me, but she was facing in the wrong direction.

"I can make myself invisible, too," Rachel said. But she couldn't. She screeched with frustration.

I tried my sleep spell again. This time, with Rachel in her natural form, it worked. Her wings stopped beating, and she dropped onto her nest, next to Sven.

He kneeled on her little body and wrapped it in a net he took from a pouch on his belt. The net automatically contracted, sealing the sprite in a cocoon.

A sweaty Sven sighed with relief and called for backup on his phone.

"I've got this under control," he said to us, unlocking the door. "Please leave the cell, and someone will let you out of the corridor."

"That was rather embarrassing," Mr. Lopez said.

257

The guard on the other side of the corridor door slid the heavy bolts one by one.

"I'm thrilled," Mrs. Lupis said with the first smile I'd seen on her. "The crested mouth sprite is a fascinating creature. I look forward to studying her."

As we walked out of the detention facility, I asked my handlers if they had their own arrangements for returning to Jellyfish Beach.

"We're riding with you," Mr. Lopez said. "We have to complete our coverup plan."

"What do you mean?"

"Making sure humans are blamed for the murders, and not the crested mouth sprite."

CHAPTER 26
LUST

"I confess I'm surprised you asked me to lunch again," Detective Shortle said, as we sat at a small table in Billy's Pizza. "Considering all you and Rosen went through."

"I'm surprised you accepted my invitation," I replied, taking a sip of my fountain soda. "I thought we'd begun a good collaboration to solve the black-magic vandalism, and it felt like a shame to throw it all away."

"What's your true motivation? You want information from me?" Shortle smiled wryly.

"Well, if you have any updates on the Umber and Carrascal investigations, I'd like to hear them. I thought the groundwork I put into them was helpful to you."

"It was. Where we stand right now . . ." She trailed off and turned her head to see who had just walked through the door.

It was a weasel-like man in a black hoody. I recognized him

as one of the Knights Simplar. He walked up to the counter and asked the attendant for the owner.

Johnny came out of the kitchen wearing chef's whites. He pulled a thick envelope from his apron pocket and handed it to the man in the hoody, who promptly left the restaurant without a word.

"That sure looked like a wad of cash, didn't it?" Shortle asked under her breath.

"It did."

"Now that Commissioner Dunot is gone, is someone new shaking down the business owners?"

"That's what it looks like." I said nothing about Ruth. It seemed best to leave the police out of it for the time being.

Johnny emerged from the kitchen again carrying a plastic tray with our two slices of pizza. He placed it on our table.

"Johnny," Shortle said. "If you're being extorted or something, please come talk to me."

"Ah, no, it's nothing like that." He fiddled with his waxed handlebar mustache. "I owed that guy some money for rims I bought for my Camaro."

Johnny wasn't a good liar. Based on Shortle's skeptical expression, she felt the same way.

"The offer to talk remains open," she said, before he walked away.

Once he was out of earshot, she leaned toward me.

"Assistant State Attorney Dreeble is confident we have enough evidence to pin the murders of Puttle and Chubb on Umber. Puttle's murder is a no-brainer; he was regularly stealing from Umber's traps and might have witnessed Umber making a drug run. Connecting Chubb and Umber was a challenge, until now."

"I told you Umber was seeing Chubb's ex-wife, and the two guys got into a fistfight."

"Yeah, but your report of the fight is hearsay. Mrs. Chubb wasn't being forthcoming, so we didn't have a witness until this weird crabber came forward."

"A guy missing his front teeth?"

"Yeah, he said he witnessed a confrontation between Charles Chubb and Umber shortly before the murder. It appears that Chubb followed his wife to the convenience store at the park in Port Inferno. Umber was there, and a big blowup ensued. It's circumstantial, but it's helpful. After all, Umber's dead, so we don't have to convict him in court."

"Are you still trying to prove that Carrascal ordered the killings?"

"No. It looks like Umber acted on his own. But we're still going after Carrascal for killing Umber. And Todd Oddbelly."

"Oddbelly? Really?"

"Yeah," Shortle said proudly. "We couldn't connect Oddbelly with Umber, but we found a connection to Carrascal."

"No way!"

"Oddbelly towed Carrascal's SUV one night from outside a restaurant. It was in a legal parking space, and towing it was a sleazy move by Oddbelly to make money. He obviously didn't know whose SUV he took."

I nodded, impressed. Strangling Oddbelly with a winch cable was something you could imagine a drug lord ordering. Even though the actual killer was a crested mouth sprite.

"Good work," I said.

I wouldn't want an innocent person charged with Rachel's crimes, but Umber was a drug smuggler and a human trafficker. Plus, he was no longer of this world and wouldn't have to serve a day in jail. Carrascal, of course, was a murderous drug lord who had a professional torturer on his payroll.

"All of this is off the record," Shortle said. "I told you, knowing full well you'll pass the information to Rosen. But tell him he can't run with any of this until he confirms it with me. As a gesture of goodwill, because of the charges wrongly brought against him, I will give him exclusive access to all developments regarding Umber and Carrascal. He'll get scoops on everything."

"I'll tell him."

AND THAT'S EXACTLY what I did after I served him dinner at my house that evening.

"What did being in jail make you crave for dinner when you got out?" I had asked him.

"A beautiful woman sitting across the table from me," he had replied. "Oh, and fresh fish."

That sounded like he wasn't harboring too much of a grudge anymore. Our solving the murders together had helped improve his mood substantially, even if the tooth fairy as culprit prevented him from writing a story about it.

He arrived at my house with a bottle of my favorite Pinot Grigio, and I presented him with a dish of baked grouper from the local fish market.

"I have to say this is better than the frozen fish sticks we got in jail," Matt said. "Especially since I'm not eating with guys who wouldn't hesitate to shiv me and take my fish sticks."

I caught him up on Shortle's attempt to solve the case without her knowing the true murderer was supernatural.

"She's going to let me get a scoop to report an incorrect story about the incorrect culprit?" he asked.

"I figured you'd say something like that."

"I've learned over the years that reporters can't make deals with the police. Sure, they can give you tips they don't give to other reporters, but they ultimately want to control you."

Despite his cynical words, the wine, good food, and pleasant dining companion seemed to be improving his mood.

"How were your first days back on the job?" I asked, thinking it was a benign question.

"Everyone in the newsroom had signed a petition demanding my release in the name of press freedom. But now that I'm back, I get the feeling they're not a hundred percent certain I'm innocent."

"Journalists are a skeptical lot."

"Yes, we are. So, what's the deal with your mother?"

"With Ruth?"

"Yeah. Sorry, I keep forgetting you don't think of her as your mother. Anyway, is she on the warpath, or is she accepting you into the coven?"

"I haven't heard from her since we escaped from her apartment."

"It sounds like my jail escape was a waste of time."

It had actually represented a big leap forward in my magical abilities, but I wisely chose not to say that.

"I expect it will lead to a reward," I said. "I just need to be patient."

"Good things come to those who wait."

I said nothing and only nodded. Because there was strange energy filling the room. As a witch, I'm highly sensitive to the various kinds of energy and how they can be best used to power magic spells.

The particular energy I was feeling was nothing I'd ever used in my magic before. Because it could only be created by the chemistry between two lovers.

Even if we weren't yet true lovers.

Though his smoldering eyes meant that being lovers was a real possibility.

As did the racing of my heart, the sweat in my hands, and the tingling in my body where it hadn't tingled in years.

"What am I feeling?" he asked in a thick voice. "Did you cast a spell on me?"

"Meet me under the table," I said.

"Where?"

"Under the table. A hurricane is coming, and we need to take shelter."

"Yes," he said, slipping from his chair and disappearing beneath the table's edge. "Time to hunker down."

I slipped off my chair, too, and met him in the shadows, away from the light of the chandelier, atop the soft Persian carpet, hidden by the tablecloth, in a little imaginary room of our own, where we could pretend we were beneath the canopy of a four-poster bed in the royal suite of a palace and dream of a future filled with endless joy and promise.

It was the best hunkering down ever.

And later, as we lay in each other's arms, staring at the bottom of the table, our sweat cooling, I didn't really mind when I heard the clicking of iguana claws on the hardwood floors near the door to the garage.

"Freaking humans!" Tony muttered before the clicking receded back into the garage.

MATT DIDN'T STAY for the night, which turned out to be a good thing, because I awoke at 2:30 a.m. to the smell of cigarette smoke and the sound of coughing coming from my living room.

And no, it wasn't Tony sneaking a puff indoors like he was forbidden to do.

"Ruth, is that you?" I called out.

"Saint Ruthless, to you, dearie."

I sighed and climbed out of bed in my oversized T-shirt and pulled on my sweatpants.

A lamp turned on in the living room as I entered, revealing Ruth sitting on the couch.

"Remember, I've asked you many times not to smoke in my house."

"'Not to smoke in my house, *your Holiness.*'"

"Look, I accept the fact you have a lot of power and a bunch of cult followers who will do whatever you want. But at the moment, you're in *my* house and must follow *my* rules. Just like here in the state of Florida, we have to follow Florida's laws."

"No, we don't. I am not bound by the laws of mortal humans."

"Last time I checked, you're human and you're mortal. And after you die, we can discuss if you're really a saint or not."

She cackled with great amusement. Which rather surprised me, because I'd expected to get hit by a lightning bolt or something.

"It's times like this that I know I'm your true mother," Ruth said. "You've got moxie, dearie. I appreciate that."

"I thought you preferred brain-dead acolytes who worship you no matter what."

"Oh, I do. But I have higher ambitions for you."

"What do you mean? I completed the tasks you gave me, even breaking Matt out of jail. And then, you betrayed me. You broke your promise to bring me into your coven. You made me your prisoner, and you tried to make Matt your slave."

"And you passed the test with flying colors."

"Huh?"

"I wanted to see what you would do. You fought back and escaped. You showed your moxie, proving that my bet on you had paid off."

"Capturing us was just a test?"

"Yes. You broke Matt out of jail, then you had to free yourself from my magic. It was your final assignment. And you completed it."

"Does this mean I can join the coven now?"

"Yes. It means you can begin your initiation process—the training and indoctrination."

"You mean brainwashing."

"That's such a crude term. But, yes."

Was it really worth joining her stupid cult to destroy it from within? Wouldn't hiring Seal Team Six to come in, guns blazing, be so much easier?

"I have lots of really cool spells to teach you," she said, like she was bribing a child with ice cream.

"Okay. What's the next step?"

"Your dues, of course. You need to pay your first two months upfront. I accept all major credit cards and digital payment methods."

I didn't hide my disgust with her mercenary nature.

"Then comes the fun stuff: the black magic! Look, dearie, you're a much better witch than the others in my coven. You're also my daughter. You will enter the coven at a higher tier than the other members. Eventually, you'll be my lieutenant. We'll be the most powerful magic team in history. And those laws you were talking about? I'll show you they're nothing but words on paper."

Infiltrating her cult was going to be a major test of my sanity.

"The next meeting is tomorrow morning, before the employed members go to their day jobs. Be there at six o'clock. And the new person has to bring donuts."

Suddenly, she was gone. I didn't even see the door open or close. It was unsettling to realize she had become more powerful than when I had tangled with her last.

I went back to bed and tried futilely to sleep. Too many questions danced in my mind.

Was it dangerous to be joining her coven? Would I be able to undermine her as Fred Furman and I had discussed, or would I slip into the dark side and become evil like her?

As if triggered by my thoughts, my left palm began to hurt. The wound I had made with the dagger to draw blood and summon Asmodeus had reopened. That made no sense; I thought it had healed.

Did summoning a demon put you in his debt? Ruth hadn't mentioned that. It would be just like her to leave out the downsides of black magic. There were undoubtedly many terrifying dangers and pitfalls, yet black magic nevertheless attracted many witches.

People who lusted for more power than they could achieve with legitimate magic.

Was I one of them?

No, I assured myself. I was just black-magic-curious—all in the name of infiltrating Ruth's cult and taking her down. Enlisting a demon to create a doppelgänger, and callously using Matt like a chess piece, were simply the costs of pursuing this mission.

Yes, I was perfectly well-intentioned, acting rationally and cautiously.

Right?

Now, I would never fall asleep. I tried to think of pleasant things, such as the many good people in my life who were a million times better than Ruth.

There was Matt, for instance. Just before I finally drifted off, I savored the memories of the warmth, and feel, and smell of him.

Was this the beginning of the commitment-free intimacy I had promised him? Or would he expect more?

Then again, perhaps I would be the one who wanted more.

Now that Ruth had gone, the cats came out from hiding and made themselves comfortable beside me on the bed. Their motto was: enjoy simple pleasures whenever you can and hide from the things that scare you.

Maybe that should be *my* motto from now on.

WHAT'S NEXT

Book Seven, Worms of Endearment, coming soon:

The worm has turned.

When Milo Fusseldink, world-renowned cryptozoologist, went missing overseas, he had been searching for the legendary Mongolian Death Worm, the Holy Grail of cryptids. I didn't think much about it at the time.

But now, people are dying here in Jellyfish Beach, Florida, victims of a rare biological poison. A toxin the legends claim is sprayed by the Mongolian Death Worm.

Of course, I get roped into investigating. And I discover a deadly rivalry in the world of monster hunting, as well as unspeakable secrets lurking in our humble seaside town.

Meanwhile, will my budding relationship with Matt blossom? Or, will one of us worm our way out of it?

Welcome to Jellyfish Beach, a wacky world of murder, magic, and mayhem.

Sign up for my newsletter

Get a free novella when you join my occasional newsletter filled with updates on new releases, special deals, and amusing content. All you have to do is visit wardparker.com

ACKNOWLEDGMENTS

I wish to thank my loyal readers, who give me a reason to write more every day. I'm especially grateful to Sharee Steinberg and Shelley Holloway for all your editing and proofreading brilliance. To my A Team (you know who you are), thanks for reading and reviewing my ARCs, as well as providing good suggestions. And to my wife, Martha, thank you for your moral support, Beta reading, and awesome graphic design!

ABOUT THE AUTHOR

Ward is also the author of the Memory Guild midlife paranormal mystery thrillers, as well as the Freaky Florida series, set in the same world as Monsters of Jellyfish Beach, with Missy, Matt, Agnes, and many other familiar characters.

Ward lives in Florida with his wife, several cats, and a demon who wishes to remain anonymous.

Connect with him on social media: Twitter (@wardparker), Facebook (wardparkerauthor), BookBub, Goodreads, or check out his books at wardparker.com

PARANORMAL BOOKS BY WARD PARKER

Freaky Florida Humorous Paranormal Novels
Snowbirds of Prey
Invasive Species
Fate Is a Witch
Gnome Coming
Going Batty
Dirty Old Manatee
Gazillions of Reptilians
Hangry as Hell (novella)
Books 1-3 Box Set

The Memory Guild Midlife Paranormal Mystery Thrillers

A Magic Touch (also available in audio)

The Psychic Touch (also available in audio)

A Wicked Touch (also available in audio)

A Haunting Touch

The Wizard's Touch

A Witchy Touch

A Faerie's Touch

The Goddess's Touch

The Vampire's Touch

An Angel's Touch

A Ghostly Touch (novella)

Books 1-3 Box Set (also available in audio)

Monsters of Jellyfish Beach Paranormal Mystery Adventures

The Golden Ghouls

Fiends With Benefits

Get Ogre Yourself

My Funny Frankenstein

Werewolf Art Thou?

In Sprite of Herself

Worms of Endearment

Made in United States
North Haven, CT
14 September 2024

57410706R00168